CHARMED

ELIZABETH ROSE

OLIVER-HEBER BOOKS

 Created with Vellum

The Sage
Isle of Denwop
Glint
Whispering Dale
Pyramids of the Gods
Quamm Caves
Asked Sea
Picajord Mountains
Macada
Kasculbough
MURA
Lake of Souls
Fae Cottage
Goeften Forest
Evandorm
Blackseed Cottage

One

EVANDORM CASTLE, LAND OF MURA

"I'll bid two chickens—still alive." Rhys Blackseed reached down, grabbing each bird by the neck, throwing them to the center of the table atop the pile of coins that had already been bet. He played cards with his brothers and the elf, Elric, out in the courtyard of his brother Zann's castle.

The chickens flapped around, causing each of the men sitting there to pull their cards closer to his chest. All three of them backed away from the fowls.

"Did you really have to do that?" grumbled Darium, the eldest of the three Blackseed brothers. He took a swig of ale and thunked the tankard down on the table, still eyeing up the pesky birds. With one hand, he pushed a strand of hair from his eyes. He had a white clump of hair that melded into the rest of his long black locks. Having a stripe atop his head was normal for a sin eater. It reminded most people of a skunet—one of the pesky black and white furry animals of Mura that left a stench wherever it went.

"Those are my chickens, you fool!" Zann said in

disgust. "Place your bid with something else. Try something that is yours instead."

"What's all the fuss about?" Rhys shrugged. "I'll pay you back if I lose. I promise. Besides, I've got better chickens at Kasculbough to replace these scrawny ones."

"My chickens are not scrawny," scoffed Zann, feeling highly insulted. After all, he was a king now, just like his brother, Rhys. Zann felt that his chickens were highly superior to those of his brother.

"Are you two done squawking or do we have to listen to both of you henpecking away all day about things that don't even matter?" Darium wanted to know.

"You're right." Zann nodded. "All right, place your bid, Darium. It's your turn now. I've got things to do and I need to end this game quickly." Zann's long blond hair was so light that it almost looked white. The color matched his shapeshifting form of a wolf. Shapeshifting was his inherited power as the second son of the Blackseed family.

"You have things to do? What things?" questioned Darium. "You're the ruler of Evandorm now, Brother. Surely, you can get someone else to do the hunting, if that's what you're referring to. You are no longer a huntsman to the king. You *are* the king," he reminded him.

True, Zann was once the huntsman for the late King Drustan Grinwald of Evandorm. But now the king was dead, and Zann filled the position of Evandorm's ruler. Reigning at his side was his new Elven Queen wife, Lira.

"But I enjoy hunting," said Zann in his defense,

looking over his shoulder at their wives who were gathered around a table filled with food. The women chatted, huddled in a circle, having planned an outdoor meal for today. "Just do me a favor and don't let Lira know, but I have urges I cannot ignore."

"Urges? What kind of urges?" Elric, who was Lira's father, ground out. The short elf climbed atop the stump he was using as a stool and put his hands on his hips, probably trying to look threatening, but everything he did was only irritating to the brothers. Elric still held on to his cards. "If I find out you're cheating on my daughter, I swear I'll have your head, Blackseed."

"Calm yourself and sit back down," said Zann with a puff of air from his mouth. "Elric, I love Lira. I also love my stepdaughter, Valindra, and our new daughter, Leandra. I would never do anything dishonorable to hurt any of them." Zann glanced over his shoulder again, smiling at his wife who waggled her fingers at him when she noticed. Little five year old Valindra was running around the courtyard, playing with Rhys' two-year-old daughter, Lily-Rae. With them were the rest of their younger cousins, Thistle, Cricket, Lucio, and Leandra.

"Good to know," sniffed Elric, slowly sitting back down. "I'd hate to think you'd be dishonorable, being a king now and all. Besides, it would be unacceptable and highly immoral. I couldn't even look at you again if I thought it were true."

"Whatever you say, Elric." Zann shook his head, not really caring what his father-by-marriage thought of him. Elric was a sage who never stopped giving the rest of them trouble, or his opinion for that matter.

When Zann found out Elric was Lira's father, he had never expected that someday the irritating little man would be related to him. His brothers found humor in the situation. Zann didn't. But for Lira's sake, he decided he'd just learn to push past this milestone and tolerate the sage and all he did.

Darium pulled a silver ring out of his pocket and slid it forward, causing the chickens to peck at it. With a swipe of his hand, he shooed the birds away. "I bid this ring."

"A silver ring? Really? Let me see that. Where did you get that?" asked Rhys, reaching out for it, but Darium slapped his hand away.

"Leave it, Rhys. It doesn't matter." Darium looked down at the cards in his hand.

"I'm just curious since I've never seen it before." Rhys stretched his neck to inspect the jewelry.

"I've never laid eyes on it either," said Zann. "Is it new, Brother? Did you perhaps buy it for Talia? If so, she won't like the fact you are using it as part of your bid."

"Nay, it's not new, it can't be," said Rhys. "Look at it. It's tarnished." Rhys pushed a chicken aside to better inspect the ring. "It's old. I'm sure of it. And it seems to have some kind of symbol in the center. It looks like a cross or something with a design around it." Rhys reached for it once more and again, Darium slapped his hand away.

"Don't worry about the damned ring," Darium grumbled. "Zann, place your bet. After all, you seem to be in a hurry and we'd hate to slow you down."

"I've seen that ring before. It looks familiar." Elric was up on his feet again atop the stump, straining his eyes, to see it. He was so short that he only reached waist high standing next to the Blackseed brothers. From a distance, most people mistook Elric for a child. Standing on things was the only way he could see what was going on, or to be noticed.

"Nay, you haven't seen it before and, no, you don't know anything about it. Now let's continue the game and stop this nonsense," growled Darium, no longer wanting to talk about the ring.

"The Sin Eater stole it from a dead man! That's what it is. Admit it, Sin Eater." Elric pointed his bony finger at Darium in accusation.

"I did not. And I'm not a Sin Eater anymore," Darium reminded him. "Well, only on occasions, but with good reason." He looked down at his cards instead of at his brothers. "You are wrong, mage, about everything, and are just trying to stir up trouble."

"I'm a sage, not a mage, and you know it." Elric stuck his pointy chin proudly in the air.

"Darium, is it true?" Rhys looked over at his older brother. "Did you steal that off of one of the dead for whom you administered your services?"

Sin Eating involved Darium being hired to eat bread and drink ale that had been placed upon the chest of a dead person who died suddenly and didn't have the time to confess their sins. Darium would thereby take on the sins of the dead so the family of the deceased would have hope that their loved one would make it to The Haven in the afterlife instead of ending up in The Dark Abyss for all eternity. Of course, the Sin Eater was then doomed for all eternity because of it, but that had been Darium's destiny, being the eldest Blackseed son. Or, at least, he thought so at the time. Since he married the fae, Talia-Glenn, and his Fae Queen mother showed up when they thought she was dead, his life now had new meaning. Things were different on Mura, especially his destiny which was no longer looking so dark.

"I did not steal the ring. For your information, Murk found it near the Quamm Caves and brought it to me." Darium's raven, Murk, swept down from the sky and landed on the table letting out a guttural cry. It strutted over to the chickens, but the fowls were too dumb to know the raven could hurt them. They curiously pecked at Murk, sending Murk flying back into the sky. "What is the problem with keeping something I found?" asked Darium.

A tsking sound came from Elric.

"What's the matter, mage?" Darium looked at the elf from the corner of his eye. "Now you think I'm dishonorable, too?"

"First of all, stop calling me a mage," said Elric in his quirky little voice. "Blackseed, it's a pity you didn't look for the owner of the ring if your bird really did find it. But what can one expect from a mere Sin Eater?"

Darium was up on his feet, ready to wring the little man's neck.

"Sit down, Darium. Don't let him rile you. He's not worth it." Zann slid a basket of slimy eggs across the table. "Here's my bid."

"Really, Brother?" Darium frowned. "Smelly Arcine eggs?" he said, speaking of the eggs of the snake-like creatures that inhabited the land of Mura. The eggs not only smelled foul but tasted just as bad, even when cooked. "Do you really think anyone wants them?"

"I told you, I don't have much time to hunt anymore since I've taken on the position of King of Evandorm, and am also a father and husband now," replied Zann shaking his head. "This is the best I can do."

"Even the damn chickens don't want to be near those stinky things, and they are used to sitting on eggs all the time." Rhys grabbed the chickens that were wandering over to the edge of the table and pushed them back to the center.

"My turn!" Elric pulled something out of his pocket and slid it across the table.

"What's that?" asked Darium, making a face.

"It's a gemstone mined by the gnomes, from the Quamm Caves."

"Gemstone? Hah!" Zann responded with a chuckle. "It looks like a simple, dirty rock to me. What are you trying to pull on us, Elric?"

"It's better than your slimy eggs!" Elric said with a sniff. "You're a king now, Zann. Why don't you bet one of your gold crowns or something of real value like the rest of us?"

"Real value?" repeated Zann. "I don't consider an old tarnished ring, two stolen chickens, and a damned rock anything of real value at all. At least my bid will fill your belly."

"Now wait a minute. The birds aren't stolen. I told you I'll replace them." Rhys picked up the rock, blowing on it and brushing it against his sleeve. "By the gods, I think it really is a gemstone like the elf said. It is shiny inside." He held up the white stone that glittered in the sun for the others to see.

"You found that in the caves?" Darium asked in interest. His eyes shot back over to the ring he'd bet. "I can't believe Murk didn't bring me one of those instead."

"There are no gemstones in the Quamm Caves." Rhys was confident with his words. "Just natural minerals and some exotic plants, that's all."

"Yes, there are and this proves it. I found it there," announced Elric proudly. "Like the rest of you, I always believed those pesky gnomes only mined stupid rocks, but now I know otherwise. And for your information, those gnomes are vicious little critters. I had to move fast and in a blur in order not to be caught." He rubbed his backside as he spoke.

"I know what you mean," mumbled Darium, rubbing his arm.

"Brother, I thought you said your crow found the ring near the caves, but you've been in the caves yourself, haven't you?" asked Zann.

"Murk is a raven, not a crow," Darium answered, his eyes still on his cards. "And I might have been near the entrance of the Quamm Caves, but what does it even matter?"

"You were inside the caves. Admit it. We all know the gnomes don't come out into the sunlight," said Rhys to prove him a liar.

"All right. So mayhap I briefly stepped inside for a minute or two, but no one can stay long with those pesky creatures living there."

"Seriously," the elf continued. "I had to zip away

using my power to move quickly to avoid their picks and axes."

"None of you should be stealing from the caves of the gnomes," said Zann. "You wouldn't like it if someone stole from your home, would you?"

"Never mind that. Elric, you must be pretty sure of winning the card game to up the bid with something so valuable," said Darium, eyeing up the elf with suspicion.

"Lay down your cards. Everyone," instructed Elric. "Let's find out who won this game once and for all."

Everyone placed their cards face up on the table. Elric let out a whoop with barely even looking at his competitors' hands. "I won, I won," he chimed, standing on the stump again and raising his arms up over his head, turning in a full circle.

"What? Nay, you couldn't have won," gasped Zann, studying the hands of cards that had been laid down.

"Let me see those cards again." Rhys inspected the elf's spread. "By golly, he did win. How in the name of Belcoum did you get such a good hand?" he asked, using the name that was referred to by some as the devil.

"That's what I want to know," said Zann, blowing a puff of air from his mouth. "You usually stink at cards, Elric. We've always been able to beat you."

"Not to mention, you were losing up until we placed these last bets," added Darium.

"I guess I'm just better at the game than you three are, after all." Still laughing and smiling, Elric reached out to scoop up his winnings. Before he could, someone walked up behind him and their hand slapped down atop his to stop him.

"He only won because he cheated," said a female voice.

The Blackseed brothers looked up to see a stranger. A beautiful woman with long black hair and piercing blue eyes stood behind the elf. She wore an aqua gown with long silk tippets that hung down well past her fingers. There was some sort of charm hanging from a chain around her neck with an odd design on it.

"He's surely cheating," the woman repeated once again. "Aren't you, Father?"

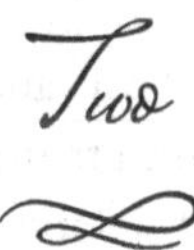

Two

Persimmon Burroughs stood before the group of men, holding down her father's hand and already wondering if she'd made a mistake by coming here to Mura.

"Did you call Elric...Father?" asked the biggest man at the table, a brute with long brown hair.

"Yes, I did," she answered, slowly releasing Elric's hand. She'd only seen her father mayhap once every five years, but he seemed just as wily and ornery as the last time they'd met. And now he looked even shorter than she remembered.

Elric glanced over his shoulder and groaned, and then sat back down. "Persimmon," he said, scrunching up his nose. "What are you doing here?"

"Before I answer that, empty your pouch," said Persimmon. "Put everything out in the open on the table where the rest of the men can see it."

"Well, time to eat." Elric got off the stump, looking as if he were about to zip away in his usual fashion. He could move faster than anyone she'd ever known. If he wanted, he could move so fast that he appeared to be nothing but a blur. She supposed it came from being an elf, but she wasn't sure. "I don't want to miss out on those pazzleberry pies that Lira made," he said.

Persimmon reached out and gripped him around the wrist now to keep him from going.

"Elric, Lira never told me she had a sister," said the man with the long blond hair and the ochre-colored eyes.

"Shhh, Zann, quiet," said Elric shaking his head, calling the man by name. It was too late. Persimmon had already heard him.

"Sister?" she repeated. "I have a sister? Father? Is this true?" Her eyes narrowed to slits as she eyed up the elf.

"All right, I confess. I cheated." Elric emptied his pouch, throwing down a few extra cards and some odd trinkets.

"Hey, that's the tooth from a Seyadillo that I got on a hunt while in my wolf form. See the hole in it?" Zann scooped it off the table. A Seyadillo was a large rodent with tough skin, so big that it was about the size of a small man. "I was planning on stringing up the tooth and wearing it around my neck. And Rhys, isn't that a tassel from your horse's tack?" Zann pointed to the trinkets Elric had emptied from his pouch.

"Is it? Let me see," said the man named Rhys, picking up the tassel and dangling it from two fingers. "Yes, it is. I've been meaning to replace that."

"This is Talia's favorite hair pin," said the man with black hair, picking up the last item to inspect it.

"She blamed me months ago for misplacing it, when you had it all along."

"They are just trinkets that I found, the same way Darium found his." Elric nodded at the dark-haired man so Persimmon knew he was called Darium.

"You had Murk bringing you his finds?" asked Darium. "I don't like that."

"Nay, I wouldn't let that dirty bird bring me anything." Elric wrinkled his nose. "I just meant that all of you must have dropped the trinkets and I found them, that's all."

"That's not it at all. You're a thief," said Zann.

"Am not," replied the elf. "Besides, they are just silly trinkets and not worth anything so what do any of you care?"

"One man's silly trinket is another man's treasure," remarked Zann, shoving the Seyadillo tooth into his pouch.

"The real issue here is that you cheated," said Rhys.

"Yes, you cheated. In more ways than one it seems." Darium scowled at Persimmon's father.

"Let's eat." Elric was ready to leave as usual. It seemed to be what he did best when he didn't want to face something. Like all the times he'd left Persimmon and her mother, just when they needed him the most.

"Nay, no one is leaving yet." Zann stood up and so did his brothers.

"We want the truth," said the big one, named Rhys. "But then, how can we really expect the truth from someone who cheats at cards?"

"That's right," said Darium with a snort. "And he had the nerve to call us dishonorable? Elric, it seems to me that you have some explaining to do. And not just about the card game either." His gaze traveled over to Persimmon when he said it.

"I agree," said Zann. "But first, let me call over my wife. Lira!" He raised his arm in the air and waved her over. One woman came to the table, followed by a few others.

"Nay, don't!" begged Elric, cringing, but it was too late. The woman named Lira and the other women in the group who had been visiting and talking, joined them.

"What is it, sweetheart?" Lira reached up and kissed her husband on the mouth. Then she noticed Persimmon standing there and her green eyes opened wide in surprise. "Oh, pardon me. I didn't know we had a guest. Hello, there. I am Queen Lira Penworth."

Her husband cleared his throat.

Her eyes flashed over to him and she grinned. "I mean Queen Lira Blackseed now," she corrected herself, blushing in a bashful manner. Her hand went to her mouth and her fingertips daintily covered her lips. "Sorry, Zann," she told her husband. "I'm still getting used to us being married."

This woman seemed to be close to Persimmon's age of twenty-five. Her beauty was beyond compare. She sported a long braid of strawberry-blonde hair trailing down her back. Her eyes were green like the new life of a spring plant. Pointy tips turned upward from the tops of her ears, a true trait of an elf. She also had a kind and bright smile. Lira was dressed in a fancy gown, depicting her noble status. And over her clothes, she wore a fur-lined long, green cloak.

"Zann, aren't you going to introduce me to our guest?"

"I would if I knew who she was," muttered Zann under his breath.

"Perhaps your father would like that honor." Darium glared at Elric. All three of the men did, actually. The air was thick between them. Persimmon could tell by the way her father shifted his weight from one foot to the other that he was feeling uncomfortable right now. So was she. This was a strange land to her since she'd never set foot on Mura before, even though she'd lived her entire life just across the water in Lornoon. Persimmon didn't know anyone here but her father, and she'd barely spoken to Elric at all while growing up. Nay, nothing here was familiar to her and neither did she feel at ease here, even if she wasn't really sure where she would feel comfortable.

Slowly, Persimmon released his arm. "Go ahead, Father. I'm sure everyone would like to hear your explanation of who I am."

"Persimmon, these are the Blackseed brothers, Zann, Rhys, and Darium," announced her father, pointing to each of the men in turn. The brothers were handsome men. Rugged and strong. Two of them were dressed like nobles and the other in clothes suited for traveling the land. "These are their wives, Lira, Medea, and Talia," he added, introducing three of the four women. Medea and Talia, just like Lira, were beautiful women. Talia was the smallest. She wore earthen-colored clothes and lilies in her hair. The strong scent of the flowers wafted through the air. Persimmon realized Talia must be a fae. Medea, on the other hand, had more exotic looks. She had long black hair like Persimmon, but dark eyes. She seemed mysterious, as if she held secrets.

"Hello," Persimmon greeted them with a quick nod.

"And last, we have the Blackseed boys' Fae Queen mother." He pointed to a woman at the back of the group.

"Persimmon's head jerked upward in surprise when she heard him say Fae Queen. Could it really be? Sure enough, she recognized the older but beautiful woman. "Oh, hello, Alai Na-Dea she said with a nod and a slight curtsy. "I am sorry, I didn't see you there. I'm surprised to find you here in Mura. I also didn't know you had sons or that you'd been crowned Queen of the Fae." She curtsied a few more times, thrilled to see the woman again after all this time, and wanting to show her respect. "It is always an honor to be in your presence, my Queen."

"Please, everyone calls me Alaina now," said the woman with a kind smile.

"Enough with all this addled talk of honor," grumbled Elric.

"There's also no need to curtsy, my dear," Alaina assured her. "We've known each other for years now, Persimmon, so we are friends. After all, I first met you when you were only a small child."

"Mother? You know her?" asked Zann. "Wait, I'm confused. How do you know each other?"

"Persimmon knows me from the time I lived with the Elementals on the island of Lornoon," explained Alaina. "I was friends with her mother, Luna. I thought I knew her well, however, I guess I was mistaken. I mean, I had no idea Elric was Persimmon's father until just now. Luna never told me."

"I see," said Zann, perusing Persimmon with a keen eye. "Can you explain more about being Elric's daughter? That, I just have to hear."

"Yes," Lira agreed with her husband. "I would like to know more, too. I have two brothers, Korack and Keevan, but I didn't know I had a sister, too. Also, you don't look like an elf. I mean, you don't have features like the rest of my family." Lira had pointy ears and light hair like any good elf had. Persimmon, on the other hand had rounded ears, dark hair, and no features depicting her as having elven blood in the least.

"I'm only half-elf," Persimmon explained. "You see, my mother was a sorceress."

"A sorceress? Really?" Medea, Rhys' wife perked up at hearing this. "Oh, it's so nice to know there is another witch around here, other than just my daughter and me."

Persimmon continued. "I don't think I really have a lot of my father's qualities at all. However, I inherited some of my mother's powers."

"Powers? What kind of powers?" asked Zann.

Persimmon looked from one person to the other, suddenly wishing she hadn't said anything. They were all strangers to her and she wasn't sure how much she wanted them to know about her. They waited with anticipation on their faces. She was going to have to tell them something now. "Well, my mother was a prophetess," she answered, being cautious not to say anything about herself.

"Oh, how exciting!" exclaimed Medea. "I knew you were special the moment I saw you. Even with all my powers, I can't say I've ever been a prophetess. It is so nice to meet you."

"You're a prophetess?" questioned Rhys. "What's that?"

"She can see the future," Medea answered before Persimmon could correct the mistake.

"Oh, you must be very powerful," gasped Talia.

"Sister, I am so proud of you. Tell us, how do you go about seeing the future?" asked Lira.

Persimmon knew she should correct them and tell her that only her mother had such a skill. As much as Persimmon longed to have the same power, she sadly didn't. It felt good to have so many people interested in her. They seemed to like her because they thought she was a prophetess. Persimmon had been sheltered her entire life. She'd never had friends, and this felt so good. Special. She wanted people to like her, and this was her perfect opportunity to start her new life. Nay, she couldn't tell them now that she wasn't a prophetess. If she did, they were all going to scorn her, and she couldn't take any more of that in her life.

"Yes. I can see the future," she blurted out, feeling like such a fake. Still, no one here knew the truth so what did it really matter? She reached over to her pouch hanging at her side, plucking out a round gazing sphere made of crystal. It was quite large and took up her entire palm. She held it up for the others to see. "I use this to scry. It used to be Mother's but it is mine now." Persimmon's gaze went to her father.

She had hoped hearing this would impress him and make him like her. Or, at least, make him a little more interested in her, since the two of them never had a bond between them.

"So that's how you knew he was cheating at cards," said Rhys with a knowing nod. "Excellent. Good work."

Persimmon liked the fact these people were admiring her and congratulating her, but guilt ate away at her gut. She couldn't back out of the lie now, but mayhap she could somehow smooth it over.

"Well, actually, no, that is not how I knew he was cheating." Persimmon told them. "You see, I didn't need to look into the crystal orb for that. I knew my father was cheating because my mother always told me that he couldn't be trusted. People don't ever change their ways, she said, and she was right as Elric has just proven." It was true her mother said this to her once, and she felt good that she hadn't just lied again. But when she saw the look on her father's face, she realized it probably wasn't a good idea to call him out like this in front of so many.

"I am not sure I agree with what you just said." Rhys took his wife's hand. "After all, Medea changed more since I first met her than you'd ever realize. She is living proof that even people with a darkness inside them can turn to the light."

Before Persimmon could ask what he meant, Lira broke in.

"Who is your mother? And where is she?" Lira stretched her neck to look around the area. "Is she here with you? I would like to meet her."

"Yes, Persimmon," said Elric in his nasal-sounding voice. "Where is Luna? She didn't come with you, did she?" Elric stretched his neck, too, trying to see over all the tall people encircling him.

Dread filled Persimmon, and sadness gripped its sharp claws into her heart. "Don't worry, Father," she answered, feeling a knot twisting in her stomach as she slid the orb back into the velvet pouch hanging from her waist belt. "Mother is not here so you won't have to face her. Actually, the only reason I sought you out at all was to tell you that she has died."

"Oh, no! I'm so sorry," Lira said with a kind look. "My mother died not that long ago. I feel your pain."

"You poor girl." Alaina rushed over and put her arm around Persimmon's shoulders to comfort her. "I knew she'd been ill, but I had no idea she has passed. I should have returned to Lornoon more often. Luna was a good woman. She will be missed by all."

"She's dead? Really?" asked the elf with little to no emotion at all in his voice. "What happened to her? Did she put a spell on the wrong person and it backfired?"

"Father!" scolded Lira. "That is highly inappropriate. Please, show a little care and compassion in this delicate situation."

"Care and compassion? Hah! It seems to me that is what got Elric into this mess to begin with," remarked Darium with a chuckle, getting a slap on the arm from his wife in return since they all knew he meant that Elric had gotten a woman pregnant.

"I admit, I might have had a fling with the witch from Lornoon, but that was a long time ago," said

Elric with a shrug of his shoulders. He acted as if it was of no importance to him, but Persimmon couldn't help noticing the way he fidgeted. It did bother him deep down. She could tell it did.

"Father, you had a relationship with another woman while Mother was still alive?" Lira's gaze quickly swept over to Persimmon before her father even had a chance to answer. "Wait a minute. How old are you, Persimmon?"

"I'm twenty-five," Persimmon answered. "How old are you?"

"I'm twenty-four, and my brothers are younger. So, Father was married to your mother before he married mine then." Lira turned toward Elric. "Why didn't you ever tell me about it? And did Mother even know?"

"Why all the questions?" Elric raised his palms. "What's done is done so what does it matter? Can we eat now?"

"Elric never married my mother," Persimmon informed them, feeling the emptiness in her life more than ever now that she was speaking to others about her mother's passing.

"Never married her?" asked Rhys.

"You had a child out of wedlock? How dishonorable," mumbled Darium under his breath.

"Do you have siblings?" asked Lira, curiously. "I have twin brothers who live in Glint, at my former castle in the elven queendom. I'd like them to meet you."

"I'd like that, too," said Persimmon, feeling a little less lonely to hear she had half-brothers along with a half-sister. "And to answer your question, no, I don't have siblings. I grew up being an only child." Her attention went to her father next. "Or should I say my mother had only me. I don't know anything about my father's immoral escapades, besides what I just found out."

Two young girls ran over. They held the hands of the other little children who couldn't have been more than a year old. The older child clung to Lira's arm. "Mother, who is that?" she asked in a small voice.

"This is your Aunt Persimmon," said Lira. "Persimmon, this is my daughter, Valindra. She is five now."

"And I'm Lily-Rae, and I'm three," said the younger girl, jumping up and down. Her fast movement scared the chickens. The birds flapped their wings, managing to scatter the cards everywhere.

"Lily-Rae, settle down," warned Rhys, picking up the little girl. "You are frightening the hens."

Before Persimmon knew what happened, a chicken was magically in the girl's arms and she was petting it.

"Put that back, honey," said her mother, taking the bird and placing it back on the table. "Our daughter has the power of transporting," Medea explained to Persimmon.

"Transporting herself, or anything else, that is," added Rhys picking up one of the younger girls. "However, our daughter, Leandra hasn't shown those powers yet."

"Oh, you have two children," said Persimmon. "How nice."

"We all do," Zann told her. "Valindra is our

daughter, and Lucio is our son." He nodded to the little boy who Lira picked up.

"And Talia and I have twins." Darium picked up one child in each arm. "Meet our son, Thistle, and our daughter, Cricket." The boy had dark hair and ebony eyes like his father, but the girl had light hair and green eyes, like most of the fae did.

"Such unusual names." Persimmon had thought her name was unique until she heard these.

"They're fae names," explained Talia.

"I see." That made Persimmon smile. She liked meeting her newfound family and finding out how unique each of them was. Persimmon's mother had been born with the power to move objects at will. Sometimes she could even conjure things from the ethers. Persimmon hadn't been born with these abilities. However, she developed the power to move things with her mind while she was growing up. "I'm happy to meet everyone. My new family, that is."

"Well, sorry you can't stay, Persimmon, but I'm sure you'll want to get back to Lornoon for the funeral." The elf left in a blur, moving so fast that no one saw where he went.

"Where did he go?" asked Persimmon, looking around.

Darium cleared his throat. "If you can't find the irritating little man, just look for the nearest pazzle-berry pie and it's a good bet you'll find him there." Darium nodded to the food table. Sure enough, there was Elric standing on his tiptoes, holding up an entire pie to his mouth.

"Father, nay!" cried out Lira, to stop him. "That

is for later. After the meal. And it is for everyone, not just you."

There came a giggle from the small girl in Rhys' arms. Suddenly the pazzleberry pie disappeared from Elric and reappeared in her hands.

"Where did my pie go?" yelled the elf, looking around, spinning in a full circle. "This isn't funny. I want pie!"

Everyone laughed.

"Give me that, Lily." Medea took the pie from her daughter, causing the little girl to cry.

"I think she's hungry," stated Rhys.

"Yes, we should all eat." Alaina motioned to Persimmon. "Won't you stay and join us for the meal?"

"I'd like that." Persimmon appreciated the kind invitation.

"I want you to show me that crystal orb later, if you don't mind." The witch, Medea, motioned with her eyes to Persimmon's pouch. "I've never seen one before and would love to know exactly how it works. You're a witch, right?"

"Yes, I am," Persimmon answered, feeling nervous admitting it since she'd had to keep it a secret for so many years now.

"We have to talk. I have so much to tell you," said Medea excitedly.

"Yes. Good. I'd like that." Persimmon cleared her throat. "Perhaps I can ask you a few questions later as well." She hoped that Medea could help her understand why her power of moving objects with her mind only appeared after she had matured. Persimmon didn't know much about being a witch since growing up she never had any real powers. Well, just one. But it was something she wasn't willing to talk about with anyone because it rather frightened her.

"Persimmon, do you have somewhere to stay now that your mother is gone?" asked Alaina.

"No, I don't," she admitted. "I am alone. I lost the house when Mother died nearly a month ago," explained Persimmon. "I couldn't pay the rent. That's why I decided to look for my father. You see, I didn't know where else to go."

"Oh, you're going to live with Elric now?" asked Alaina.

"I'm not sure." Persimmon felt a heaviness in her heart. "I'm afraid my father never wanted anything to do with me. I highly doubt that he'll allow me to stay here with him now. You see, I barely know him. I'm not even sure I really should have come to Mura at all."

"Nonsense," said Lira, overhearing her and breaking into the conversation. "You are of my blood and you will live with me from now on."

"In the Elven Queendom?" she asked, feeling intrigued and almost liking the idea for a moment. She didn't know much at all about elves but would love to learn all about them since she was part elf, too.

"Nay, not in Glint. I'm talking about right here on this side of the mountain. At Evandorm Castle." Lira motioned with her arm to the grand castle before them.

The kingdom was on the southeast end of Mura, and butted up to the Masked Sea. Persimmon had caught a ride on a boat with a tradesman from Lornoon. That is why she ended up here instead of on the other side of Mura. Evandorm had a cropping of small buildings and homes inside the protection of the castle walls. The villagers set up stalls in front of their homes which she imagined was for selling and trading their wares to others in Mura or tradesmen from different lands that came to visit. It seemed to be such a happy place to live. So colorful and lively. A cobblestone courtyard led from the large keep, and in the center of the courtyard was a tall, bubbling fountain filled with wild birds that came to drink. It felt safe and comfortable here. It was a true honor to be asked to stay, and she wasn't about to refuse the offer. However, she still had so many questions about Mura and things she did not understand.

"I'm confused," said Persimmon. "So, Lira, you are queen of two castles then? Evandorm and the Elven Queendom of Glint?"

"Nay, just one. I gave up my throne at Glint to my Aunt Sasha when I married Zann," explained Lira. "I am Zann's wife now, and he is King of Evandorm. So this is my new home."

"How interesting," said Persimmon, not understanding how any woman could give up her throne and her entire queendom for a mere man.

"Will you please stay?" asked Lira, excitement growing in her eyes. "I'd love for us to get to know each other better. After all, we are sisters. I've never had a sister before, and we have so much to catch up on."

"Yes. Yes, we do." Persimmon felt a restlessness deep inside her. This wasn't her home. Not really. Then again, she had no home anymore, so what would it matter where she laid her head? Even back in Lornoon, she hadn't lived with her mother. If she would have had her way, she would have stayed close to her mother and never left her side. But, unfortunately, that is not what happened. "Yes, sister. I'd be happy to stay with you at Evandorm Castle. It would be an honor," she told Lira, getting a feeling without even attempting to use her gazing crystal that something dangerous was about to happen in her life.

Three

Stone Nightstalker dismounted his horse and cautiously got down on his knees, still gripping his crossbow, ready to use it at the spur of a moment. He was always aware of every noise and motion around him. It was his ability to be so observant that landed him the job of the king's bounty hunter in the first place. He spotted something on the ground in the dark. Something that could possibly lead him right to the man he was tracking. His dog, Fang, sniffed the area around them, and trailed off in a different direction.

"Did you find something?" asked his good friend, Aithrod in a low voice. He dismounted his steed and wrapped the reins around a branch of a tree. Aithrod was a loner, same as Stone. Neither one of them had family left anymore on Taelgonoth. The past few years had been hard.

It was a dark night with only a crescent moon gracing the sky. Clouds passed over the scant light, leaving the normal man blind to his surroundings. Darkness never bothered Stone. He had the night sight of an animal, able to see in light or dark, it didn't matter. He liked the skill. It was a true asset in his profession. His father before him used to have excellent eyesight as well.

"I did find something," Stone answered, slowly removing one leather gauntlet and using two fingers to pick up a small stone. There were footprints in the soft dirt right beside it. Bringing the rock up to his face, he shifted it back and forth, blowing off the dust. Sure enough, a faint glimmer of green emerged from the stone.

"What is it?" Aithrod, with his eyes glancing back and forth, hurried over and hunkered down next to Stone. Aithrod was a good friend. Actually, Stone's only friend. Stone and Aithrod had grown up together, their fathers being friends as well. Aithrod joined Stone a few years ago to do bounty hunting for King Helix Kapion of Taelgonoth after the deaths of their families from a plague.

Aithrod held a tall staff that was Stone's. It was his weapon of choice. Stone was a fighter, not a murderer. He liked to bring back the fugitives alive, unarmed and unharmed. King Kapion saw to their punishments. Or their executions. Aithrod was there only as Stone's helper but had learned from Stone many of his tracking ways. Plus, the man was the only person Stone really trusted.

The king, among others, had told Stone that he was the best bounty hunter, not only this side of the Marion Marshes or in the Brackens Forest, but in all the land of Taelgonoth. He was a nightstalker, as his family surname implied. That is, he hunted usually by night because that is what he preferred. It gave him an advantage since that is when most thieves and bandits came out. Stalking bandits, thieves, and even strange creatures at times, Stone's work never ended.

Not here.

Not in a land filled with treachery and deceit.

Taelgonoth wasn't always a filthy, backstabbing, demoralizing place to live. But since the recent plague, everyone and everything changed for the worse. People panicked. Riots and looting were a common thing, since everyone always seemed to want more.

The days when goodness outweighed the bad were gone. Stone's late father had once helped the king by keeping order in Taelgonoth. His father, Stewart Nightstalker, as well as Stone and Stone's late brothers had been a strong team when they worked together. With them working together to conquer the bad, Taelgonoth had been a fair and just place to live. But not anymore. There were so many murders and robberies as of late that there was no resting for Stone and Aithrod. Even the king had turned deceitful lately. Still, he was the only hope of bringing the land back to what it once was before all the troubling times.

Stone's work pleased King Helix. So much so that he told Stone after this mission, Stone would be betrothed to his daughter, Annabelle. Since Stone no longer had a family and was twenty-eight and unmarried, he figured this would be a good move for him. He'd settle down and have children and teach them his trade. He barely knew the girl, but as soon as he returned successful from this mission, that would all change. He'd be married, and live at the castle with the nobles. The king might even possibly give him a permanent position at court. It would never replace the family he'd lost, of course, but it would give him somewhere to be settled and to call home.

"I found one of the king's stolen gems as well as the footprints of our thief." Stone glanced down to study the evidence of where the thief walked. "It looks like there are two of them. I don't see hoof-prints so they must be on foot. And I know these prints."

"What do you mean?" asked Aithrod.

"I recognize the odd soles of the man's shoes. It is Rancor Ruse we are tracking. I'm sure of it."

Rancor was one of the biggest thieves in Taelgo-noth. And also Stone's biggest enemy.

"Rancor. It figures," said Aithrod. "Well, at least they're on foot so it will slow them down and enable us to catch them faster."

This wouldn't be the first time they hunted down this crook. Stone had managed twice before to bring Rancor back to the king. But somehow the man always seemed to escape before he could be imprisoned.

Stone glanced upward next, scoping out the horizon. "They are probably hiding with the gemstones in one of these caves." He inspected the footprints more closely. He opened his pouch and dropped the gem into it, and then replaced his glove.

"Well, there are plenty of caves in Taelgonoth. Which one should we search first?" asked Aithrod.

Stone surveyed the footprints that led to the closest cave.

"Rancor is a weasel and a thief. He has stolen money from everyone through the years. However, this time he's gone for royal jewels." Stone secured the reins of his horse loosely to a tree. Then he started in the direction of the footprints. "He can't really be planning on staying in Taelgonoth. He must plan to leave here. But, oddly, he's not heading for the water and a boat."

"How can you be sure he wants to leave?" asked Aithrod.

"He'd never be able to sell the jewels. Not when everyone knows they belong to the king. Plus, he knows I'll find him sooner or later. Nay, he's leaving. I'm sure of it."

"But where would he go?" Aithrod was right behind him.

"Come, Fang," Stone called his huge white hound. The animal looked more like a wolf than a dog. Fang came running over to him, skidding to a halt at Stone's side.

"A mysterious hooded man has been seen lurking around town the past few days," reported Aithrod. "The townsfolk fear for their children and their belongings. He goes from house to house, taking what he wants. What he needs. His face is always covered. He's also said to have an accomplice."

"Yes," agreed Stone. "The second set of footprints. Have you heard if Rancor has killed or hurt anyone?"

"Not that I know of," answered Stone's friend.

"What are the reports of what he's stolen from the commoners?"

"Mostly food and clothes." Aithrod shrugged. "I wonder why he hasn't stolen horses."

"Because he knows he won't be able to use them or take them wherever he is planning to go."

"You might be right. He's planning on leaving Taelgonoth with the king's riches and selling them perhaps across the sea. Still, he could have used horses to get there. This makes no sense at all. If he is trying to escape Taelgonoth, then why head for the caves?"

"Rancor is up to something. Something different than what he usually does," said Stone. "We need to find him and his counterpart and bring them to justice as quickly as possible. With each day that passes and the king's gems missing, the people are going to start losing faith in their sovereign. King Helix will lose all respect. Or what little is left of it. Attackers might even try taking over the castle if word gets out that his security is weak and lacking."

They approached the cave and Stone led the way inside. Fang pitter-pattered past him, sniffing around in the night. It was dark and damp as caves usually are. It was also strange that the footprints just suddenly stopped right inside the entrance. And where they stopped was a dry and scorched area on the cave floor.

"This is odd." Stone hunkered down to inspect the scorch marks while Fang sniffed around scratching at the cave floor. When Stone leaned in closer, he felt a blast of heat hit his face. The air in front of him quickly changed from cool to dangerously hot. He jumped up in surprise.

"Something's happening," Aithrod called out. "I don't understand what it is but I am starting to see something appear." Aithrod rubbed his eyes in disbelief.

Stone saw it, too, and stumbled backwards. Colors of blue, pink and orange appeared inside the cave, creating a circular motion that kept expanding. The light formed an egglike shape that grew taller and wider until it was large enough to encompass a person. It was accompanied by a strange sound like metal scraping against metal. An acrid stench of something burning filled the air. It caused a shiver to run up his spine. Stone had never experienced anything like this before. He had no idea what it could possibly be. As the sound grew louder, he and Aithrod had no choice but to cover their ears.

"I could be wrong, but I think it's a portal opening up," Stone shouted, not able to believe his eyes. Fang stood next to him, barking furiously at the unseen foe.

"A what?" asked Aithrod, cringing from the sound, his hands still over his ears.

"Be on your guard. I'm not sure what might come through." With his crossbow over his shoulder, Stone grabbed his fighting staff from his friend. Aithrod yanked a dagger from his waist belt, holding it out in front of him for protection. Fang's head lowered. With a deep growl, the dog showed its teeth.

"I don't see anyone coming through," yelled Aithrod.

Stone squinted his eyes, thinking he saw rocks or a cave on the other side. For a mere second he even thought that he saw movement, but he couldn't be sure. "Neither do I," Stone answered. "But I think I know where our thief has disappeared to. Follow me."

"Wait! What are you doing, Stone? You're not really going to step through that thing, are you?" Aithrod shook his head. "You're crazy. We have no idea what might happen or even to where it leads."

"Stay if you'd like, but I'm going through. Come on, Fang," he commanded his hound. Stone first reached out with his staff, seeing the end of it disappear into the swirling portal. Then he carefully stepped forward, and walked through the opening with his dog following on his heels.

Immediately, a swishing noise filled Stone's ears. He was sucked forward through the portal, being thrown from side to side. It was as if a huge breeze toyed with him like a leaf in the wind. His knees buckled and he felt his body being tossed around like a doll. He hit the ground hard. Rolling and dropping his staff, it clunked against the stone floor before it rolled just out of his reach. Fang landed next to him yelping, his feet still running in midair.

"Aaaaaah," he heard Aithrod scream from behind him, still inside the portal. Stone quickly rolled out of the way just as his good friend hit the ground next to him. Fang reached down and licked Aithrod's face.

"Thanks," grumbled Aithrod. "But that doesn't help much, Fang. It was a hard landing." Aithrod gently pushed the dog away and rubbed his shoulder.

Then, there was that sucking sound again. Just as fast as the portal opened, it snapped shut and disappeared from sight.

"Damn! It's gone," gasped Aithrod. "And now, we're stuck here. Wherever here is." He looked around the dark cave.

"It'll open again. Somehow. I hope." Stone got to his knees.

"Where are we?" Aithrod lie on his back, staring up at Stone.

"I'm not quite sure." Stone took a moment to

look around, brushing off his clothes at the same time. Spying his staff on the floor of this cave-like structure, he walked over and bent down to pick it up. But when he did, a sharp pricking feeling stabbed him on the backside. He grabbed the staff, whirling around, thinking it was the dog.

"Stop that, Fang!" Instead of his hound, he saw a group of small, strange beings no taller than his knees. They peered up at him, seeming leery of Stone's arrival. These cave-dwellers were human-like, but much, much smaller. The lot of them seemed to be a mixture of both men and women. They all wore tall, colorful pointed hats. "What the hell," he grumbled, getting another poke on the backside, and spinning around to discover that they were surrounded on all sides by these little people. The men all had long white beards. The women wore long gowns and were round and busty. Fang sniffed the air, half wagging his tail, not sure if they were friendly and wanted to play or if they were a threat. Then the dog stopped and hunkered down and let out a slight growl.

"Stone, what's going on?" Aithrod jumped up, holding out the tip of his dagger. "Back! Back, I say," he spoke to the small beings who were closing in on them.

"They're armed. Sort of," said Stone, noticing that each of them held on to what looked like a rake, a hoe, or a shovel. Some even held sharp pick axes and pitchforks. Now he knew what they'd pricked him with, and he didn't like it in the least.

The small ones spoke in grunts to each other, and their communication was very fast. It sounded like gibberish to him. Stone tried hard but couldn't make out actual words. Then they started moving forward with their weapons drawn, closing in on both the men and the dog.

"I get a bad feeling about this." Aithrod waved his dagger back and forth.

"I don't think they'll really harm us," said Stone. "After all, they're so small. I mean how could they be an actual threat to someone our size? Hello there," said Stone, bending over and reaching out for a shake. "Ow!" he shouted when one of the creatures brought the sharp end of his hoe down across the back of his hand, actually drawing blood. Half a dozen of them jumped onto Stone's back next. He whirled around in circles throwing them off with the force.

The little peoples' grunting became louder and louder. Then even more of them appeared, filling the cave area completely. He had never seen anything like it in his life.

"Got any ideas how to escape them?" asked Aithrod as their situation worsened.

"Not a one," Stone answered with a shake of his head. "I'm afraid this is beyond my bounty hunting abilities. And for the life of me, I don't know what the hell they are, or for that matter where we are." He gripped his staff tightly as he and Aithrod continued to back away. "Get ready to fight," said Stone, not wanting to hurt these creatures, but not knowing what they were capable of doing. "I suddenly get the feeling that mayhap we shouldn't have stepped through the portal after all."

* * *

"May I please see your gazing sphere, Persimmon?" Medea, the other woman who was a witch, held out her hand as everyone sat around the outdoor fire chatting. The meal had been a fine one consisting of strange meats, vegetables and fruits that Persimmon had never had before. One of the best things she'd tasted was called Roakan. She was told that the deer-like animal had been hunted in the elven lands of Glint. It was all delicious to her. And what made the meal even better was that everyone was so friendly. Thankfully, she had been accepted by these people here on Mura. Everyone, that is, but her father.

Elric had gone out of his way to purposely avoid her and to not even speak to her since she'd gotten here. Persimmon didn't understand his actions. It really upset her. After all, she was his daughter, just as Lira was. So why did he treat the elven queen much better than he did her? It was getting dark now as the sun set on the horizon. She was told that the children of the Blackseed brothers would need to be put to bed for the night soon.

"I'm sorry, Medea, but I don't let anyone touch my gazing sphere." Persimmon was protective over the orb for more reasons than one. "My mother always told me not to let others' touch our tools. I guess it is because of the risk of their energy entering the object."

"Is that a bad thing?" asked Medea.

"Yes. No," she corrected herself not wanting to offend Medea. "I mean, I think it could be a distraction if nothing else, I suppose. Anyway, the orb only responds to my touch." The last thing Persimmon wanted to do was to show Medea how it worked, because, she honestly didn't know. She'd let them believe she saw visions in it, but that was the furthest thing from the truth. She was extremely tired of not having the ability to scry. It was draining and made her feel like a failure. After all, if her mother had been a prophetess, she should be able to do it, too.

Persimmon had yet to see anything at all in the orb. Still, things just had to change soon Her mother had used this same orb to scry, and had so much success, people sought her out from near and far to scry for them.

"Oh, I see." Medea looked extremely disappointed by her response, even though she was too polite to say so.

Persimmon felt bad now. The witch girl had been excited about seeing the orb. She also seemed to want to be Persimmon's friend. That would be nice. Persimmon never had any true friends. Since they were both witches, that should create a bond.

"I'll tell you what," said Persimmon. "I will let you look at the orb if you'd like. Without touching it, of course." She brought the orb out of her pouch, setting it in front of Medea atop the table.

"Thank you. Oh, my. It's splendid." Medea's eyes lit up in excitement. "Now show me how you make it work. Please," she begged. "I promise I won't touch it. I'll just watch as you scry."

"I...I can't do that," said Persimmon with her hand still on the orb. She was put in an awkward situation and wasn't sure how to handle it. She couldn't let on that she didn't have the magical skills to actually use the orb.

"Oh, is that forbidden, too? Letting anyone

watch you scry?" asked Medea with a sigh. "This is much different from my witchcraft. I can see that now."

"Nay, that's not it at all. I mean, I don't think it is forbidden." Persimmon didn't know what to say. Still, she needed to say something. If not, she was sure that Medea wouldn't stop until she was satisfied by getting an answer. "I can't explain how to use it because I don't understand exactly how it works. It just does." Persimmon's gaze flashed over to her father sitting at the other end of the table. Elric scowled at her. Then he got off the stump and in a flash he disappeared. "Why doesn't he like me?" she said aloud.

"Who?" Medea turned around to look, but the elf was already gone.

"Elric. My father," said Persimmon. "He acts as if I'm poison. He doesn't want to be near me or even talk with me at all. I don't understand what I ever did to make him act that way."

"Oh, that." Medea laughed. "Don't take it personally, Persimmon. Elric is quite odd if you haven't noticed. None of us can quite figure him out so we've stopped trying."

"What do you mean?" she asked.

"His own daughter, your sister, Lira, banished him from her castle in Glint years ago. That's why he's lived by himself up at the top of a cliff, so I'm told. He is extremely eccentric and not the best at being sociable."

"She banished him from the castle? That is odd. You're right." Persimmon released a deep breath and forced a smile. "There are so many things I need to learn about this land. I also have so much I want to ask my father. Through the years as I was growing up, I never had the chance."

"Why not?" asked Medea. "Was it because he was here in Mura instead of by you in Lornoon?"

"Well, that is part of the reason."

"I'm so sorry, sister." Lira overheard them, hurrying over and sitting down on the bench next to Persimmon, putting her hand over hers. "My father isn't the easiest person to get along with. Just ask my husband, Zann, and his brothers if you don't believe me."

"Lira is right," agreed Medea. "Elric hasn't always been kind to them, but our husbands have learned to tolerate the little man. Even when he continues to constantly call them big oafs."

"But Zann married you," said Persimmon, not quite understanding. "He knew Elric would be his father by marriage and yet he still went through with the wedding?"

Lira giggled. "It wasn't really his choice."

"What do you mean?"

"We were tricked into getting married. By my father. Our father," Lira explained.

"Tricked into marriage? Why? I don't understand. Do you mean you didn't want to marry Zann?"

"Don't get me wrong," Lira said, holding up her hand. "Zann and I fell in love eventually and now we couldn't be happier together. So, you see, it all worked out in the end."

"I don't really see, but I suppose I shouldn't try to understand," answered Persimmon, starting to know what they meant about ignoring Elric's odd actions. Mayhap she was getting much too upset by something that she couldn't control.

"Sweetheart, I think our little princess needs you," Zann called out, rocking their one-year-old baby, Leandra, who wouldn't stop crying.

"Excuse me, Persimmon, but I need to go to my daughter." Lira got up to leave. "When you are ready to sleep, come into the castle and we'll find you a room."

"We really should leave now, too, Medea." Rhys walked up holding the hand of their daughter, Lily. He held their son, Lucio, in the crook of his other arm. The little boy was already sleeping against his chest.

"Leave so soon?" asked Medea. "But I haven't had time yet to talk about witch things with Persimmon. I'm excited to have her here in Mura."

"You will have plenty of time for chatting later," said Rhys with a shake of his head, motioning to his wife to go.

"Goodbye, Persimmon. We're glad to meet you." The fae, Talia, had her daughter, Cricket, in her arms. Her husband, Darium, held their sleeping son, Thistle. "The children need their rest or they'll be cranky come morning."

"Don't all of you live here at Evandorm Castle?" Persimmon wanted to know.

"Nay, of course, not," said Rhys. "Medea and I have our own castle nearby."

"It's called Kasculbough Castle," explained Medea, getting up and taking Lily-Rae's hand. "Mayhap you can come stay with us on the morrow?

Then we'll have more time to visit and get to know each other better."

"Perhaps I will. Yes, that would be nice, thank you," answered Persimmon, picking up her crystal orb. When she did, for a quick second she thought she saw a flash from the corner of her eye, coming from the ball. It happened so fast that she couldn't be sure. "That's odd," she commented out loud.

"What's odd?" asked Medea, straining her neck to see the gazing ball.

"I'm sure it's nothing." Persimmon thought she must have imagined it since she wanted so desperately to see visions in the ball the way her mother always had. She quickly tucked the magical orb back into her pouch.

"Nay, tell me. It's all right. What did you see?" Medea pressed her to answer.

"It was just a flash of swirling colors. I'm sure it didn't mean a thing." She wasn't sure why she'd just admitted that aloud. Perhaps it was because she needed someone to talk to and was tired of being alone.

"Swirling colors?" asked Talia. "Darium, that almost sounds like—"

"Nay, it's nothing. Let's go," Darium stopped her in mid-sentence.

"Uh, oh," said Rhys. "I hope it's not what I think it is."

"It's not," said Darium in a firm voice. "Just ignore it. All of you."

"It's not what?" Persimmon stood up and stifled a yawn.

"The men are afraid it's another portal that you've glimpsed," explained Lira.

"A what?" she asked, thinking this sounded odd indeed.

"Did I hear someone say portal?" Zann walked over with the crying baby in his arms. Their older daughter, Valindra ran over to her mother's side.

"I'm scared, Mother," cried Valindra. "I don't like portals. They frighten me." She looked around with wide eyes and clung to her mother's gown.

"What's going on?" asked Persimmon, realizing the word portal seemed to put everyone on edge.

No one answered. Persimmon felt very uncomfortable so decided to change the subject. "Darium and Talia, perhaps I can come stay at your castle too, since I'd like to see where all of my new family lives."

"I'm sorry, but we don't have a castle," answered Talia. "Just a cottage in the woods in the Goeften Forest."

"It's a fine cottage, but small," said Darium. "It wouldn't be comfortable for you to stay with us. It is already tight with the two children. Why don't you just stay with my brothers since they have more room. Let's go, wife." Darium seemed embarrassed or put out in some manner because he didn't have a castle like his brothers. He hurriedly ushered his family to the waiting horse and wagon.

"I'm sorry if I said something wrong." Persimmon felt genuinely bad.

"Oh, don't worry, you didn't," answered Medea. "Darium will get over it. Eventually."

"Mother, I want to go home," whined little Lily.

"I agree. Take my hand, Lily," said Rhys. "Lucio and I will go home with you."

"Nay, wait. I'll come, too. See you on the morrow, Persimmon." Medea grabbed Lily's other hand, connecting her whole family in one line. Then, in a flash, they all just disappeared.

"Oh!" exclaimed Persimmon, not used to seeing this. "How do they do that?"

"You'll get used to their transporting ability in time," Lira told her. "The rest of us walk or take horses to get where we want to go. However, they don't need to do so. It's very convenient and quick to just dissipate and reappear somewhere else."

"Then, not everyone on Mura can do that?"

"Nay, of course not. Only the witches," said Zann. "By witches, I mean Medea and her daughter, Lily."

"But I saw Rhys and Lucio disappear, too. Are they also witches?" asked Persimmon.

"No, they are mortals," explained Lira. "But Medea and Lily can take others with them when they transport. "Sister, would you like me to show you to your room now? It is getting late."

"Yes, please," said Persimmon.

"Where are your bags? Your things?"

"I don't have any," she told her, not wanting to explain why."

"All right then." Lira turned to lead the way.

Persimmon felt as if she were being watched from behind. When she looked over her shoulder, she saw her father in the shadows. Then in a blur of color, he was gone, not unlike the transporting that Medea and her daughter could do.

"Everyone comes and goes so quickly here on Mura," commented Persimmon as they headed to the castle.

"There is a lot happening here. You won't be able to learn about everyone and everything in one night," Lira told her. "We are glad you decided to live here now, because there are a lot of people to meet and a lot to experience."

"I'm sure there is." Persimmon looked down at her pouch, still feeling like a failure and now a liar, too. "I can't wait for someone to explain more to me about these portals," she said, not wanting to think about the gazing orb and what had happened.

She saw their daughter cringe when she said it.

"It's best not to mention them around the children or my husband and his brothers," whispered Lira. "Excuse us now." Lira, took the baby from Zann, letting Valindra pull her away as they headed into the castle.

After they left, Zann spoke to her. "She's right, you know."

"What do you mean?" asked Persimmon.

"Don't even mention portals again," Zann warned her, crossing his arms over his chest.

"I'm sorry, but I don't understand. Why is everyone acting so odd about this?"

"It's been over a year now since any portals opened on Mura, and we want to keep it that way. Every time one opens, it means trouble for all involved. Not only trouble, but people end up dying."

"Oh, nay! They do? So it's happened a lot then?"

"Not a lot, but too much. And it is better that it doesn't happen again."

"Do you think that was a portal I saw in my gazing orb?" she asked Zann.

"Nay!" Zann didn't seem to want to even entertain the idea that it possibly could have been.

"My mother always told me that the gazing crystal is never wrong." Since this was the first time she actually saw anything inside the orb, Persimmon felt excited and wanted to see more than just a flash. Still, she didn't feel as if she could talk to anyone about it. Especially since she wasn't convinced that it hadn't just been her imagination and that she hadn't scried at all.

"It's never wrong, you say?" Zann raised a brow. "If that is so, then throw the damned orb into the Lake of Souls so you don't ever see such things again. And whatever you do, be sure not to even mention what you saw again. Never, and I repeat never, mention the word portal again."

Four

"Put him down, Fang," commanded Stone, seeing his dog with a struggling little man in his jaws. "We are not here to hurt or kill anyone."

"Ow! Really?" Aithrod, used his foot to scrape one of these cave-dwelling beings off his leg as the thing started to crawl up him. "Because right now, I'm so hungry that I'm ready to make a meal out of most of them."

"Make your way to the mouth of the cave." Stone used his staff to push the creatures aside. He still felt the pricks of their hoes and shovels at his back but tried to ignore them. He didn't want to hurt them, so he refrained from drawing his sword or using his crossbow. "I have a feeling this is their home and they consider us trespassers."

Just as he said that, a group of them rappelled down from the ceiling using ropes, with more ropes in their hands. They quickly wound them around Stone.

"Nay! Get off of me," Stone yelled. "I don't want

to hurt you but I swear I will if I have to." He pulled at the ropes and pushed at the creatures. Fang barked furiously and snapped at the air. Thankfully, that scared the little people, making them pull back a little.

"Run while you still can!" shouted Aithrod, dashing for the mouth of the cave with an army of the cave-dwelling beings whooping and waving their weapons right behind him. They not only kept up with him, but passed him up, circling back around him.

Just when Stone thought they had no chance of getting out of here without killing some of them, someone else appeared in the cave. He saw a flash or blur of color, and a small man with pointy ears like an elf stopped in front of him with his hands on his hips. He had a pouch filled with something hanging at his side. This man was about waist-high to Stone, but twice the height of the cave-dwellers. This one reminded Stone of an elf.

"Who are you and what are you doing in this cave?" the man demanded to know. His voice was high and nasal sounding.

"Oh, nay. They're growing in size," Stone called out to his friend. Fang lunged for the man, but the elf was too fast for the dog. The elf zipped around in a blur, ending up sitting on Fang's back, yanking at his ears.

"Leave my dog alone!" shouted Stone, holding out his staff, meaning to knock the man off the dog's back if needed.

"Balderdash! What are you all doing here in my cave?" The elf was thrown off when Fang shook. The man landed on a stone ledge. When he did, his pouch fell from his belt. Lots of rocks fell out. Stone realized that these rocks looked very familiar. Especially since they were sort of sparkling a little.

"I've seen those stones before." Stone pulled another three of the cave people off of him. "Can't you make these things stop attacking us?"

"They're gnomes, and, nay, I can't," said the elf nonchalantly. "They have minds of their own. I don't control them."

"I thought you said this was your cave. So tell them to leave."

"It's not that simple, fool." The elf scooped up the stones and slipped them back into his pouch. "And what do you mean you've seen these stones before? I just discovered them in this cave, and I can assure you they are not found naturally here."

"Arrrgh," moaned Stone, pulling more gnomes from him, feeling their weapons hitting harder.

"Tell me!" commanded the elf. "Where have you seen these stones before?"

"I have a stone just like that in my pouch," Stone answered.

"You stole it from me!" The little man accused him, pointing at him with one gnarly finger.

"Nay, I didn't. I found it on the other side." Stone looked up to see Aithrod just about at the mouth of the cave. Fang ran in circles barking, snapping at the gnomes that continued to poke at him. The dog put down his head and tossed one of the small men with the pointed hats high into the air. The gnome made a squealing sound and his friends ran forward to catch him.

"Other side? Other side of what?" asked the elf in his high and mighty tone.

"Get us out of here and away from these gnomes and I'll tell you what you want to know," said Stone, trying to make a deal to be free of these pesky creatures.

"Oh, for Zoroct's sake!" The elf sped around the room so fast that the gnomes couldn't catch him. It took the attention off of Stone so he and his hound were able to make it to the opening of the cave.

"Hurry, Fang," Stone commanded his dog as he and Aithrod stumbled out of the cave and into the sunshine.

"Aaah!" Aithrod held up a hand to cover his eyes from the bright light. Since the gnomes weren't following them, they plopped down on the ground in the sand to rest. They seemed to be on some sort of beach. There was a sea of water nearby with waves crashing against the rocks and rolling onto the shore. Fang ran over to join them, turning to get in a few more barks at the troublesome gnomes that were no longer there.

"We're free," said Stone, wiping his brow and trying to catch his breath. Fang lay down by his feet.

"It's already morning?" asked Aithrod. "It was night when we left. How long were we in there?"

"I didn't think it was that long," Stone answered, shading his eyes with his hand and looking up at the sun. "And it seems more like midday than morning if you ask me. That's odd. I have a feeling we are far from home."

"All right, fess up."

Stone jerked backward as the elf appeared,

perching himself atop a rock right above Stone's head.

"What are you talking about?" asked Stone.

"Tell me where you got that gemstone. And let me see it, too."

"Slow down, little fellow," said Stone with a chuckle.

Before he knew what happened, the elf was right next to him, glaring at him with narrowed eyes and his long, pointy nose.

"Don't call me little fellow. Ever! My name is Elric. I am a sage and deserve your respect. And for that matter, who in Belcoum's name are you?" He looked at Stone and Aithrod, as he backed away from the panting dog.

"I'm Stone Nightstalker," he answered. "Although I have no idea who Belcoum is."

"Hmmph. Fitting name for a stone stealer, I suppose. And Belcoum is what some of you from different lands call the devil." The elf's open palm shot forward. "Give it to me. Come on, come on, hand it over."

"I'm his friend, Aithrod Gabbencort, in case you're wondering. And Stone's dog's name is Fang," Aithrod said from the ground next to them.

"I wasn't wondering and neither do I care. Now come on, Stonestealer. I'm waiting." The elf's toe tapped the ground impatiently.

"Stone Nightstalker," he corrected him, shaking his head. "All right. Fine, I'll show it to you since you did help us escape the gnomes." Stone reached for his pouch. "By the way, what is this place called that we're in?"

"What do you mean?" asked Elric.

"We have no idea where we are," Aithrod explained.

"You don't know about the Quamm Caves?" asked Elric. "Any fool knows not to go in there unless you want to be attacked by gnomes."

"Nay, I meant the land. This whole area," said Stone, digging the gemstone out of his pouch.

"How can you not know where you are? You don't remember where you were going?"

"Well, it wasn't our choice to be in those gnome caves to begin with," said Aithrod, with a puff of air from his mouth. "We were in there because that is where the portal took us."

"Did you say, portal?" The elf's hand slowly lowered to his side. "Are you telling me that you came through a portal?"

"That's what he said. How can you not listen to what we say?" answered Stone, not caring that he was being cocky with the elf. Let him taste a little of his own medicine.

"From where?" the elf demanded to know. "Where were you before you came through the portal?"

"We were home. In our land of Taelgonoth." Stone got to his feet. "I'm sure you've heard of it. Now please tell us what land we are in and how to get back."

"Nope. I've never heard of Taelgonoth," answered Elric, even though Stone didn't believe him. "And you are in Mura, you big oaf. Just go back home the same way you came."

"Did you say, Mura?" asked Aithrod, getting to

his feet as well. The dog did so, too, and hurried behind a large rock to lift his leg. "I don't know of any land named Mura, do you, Stone?"

"Nay, I don't." Stone shook his head. "And since it was the middle of the night when we walked through the portal and now it looks to be midday, I'd say our lands are far from each other."

"Don't know, don't care. Now let me see my gem, and then I'll be on my way." The elf's open hand shot out again.

Stone held up the rock, ready to let Elric see it, but something told him he couldn't trust him so he held back. He pulled his hand away and lifted up the rock between two fingers. "There," he said. "You see, it has a slight sparkle like yours do. It was stolen from the King of Taelgonoth and needs to be returned along with the rest of them."

The elf tried to take it, but Stone was ready for him and snapped close his hand and pulled it away.

"What is your king's name?" asked the little man, squinting one eye as he perused them.

"King Helix Kapion," Aithrod told him.

Elric's eyes opened wide, then closed to slits. He seemed to be furious about something. "Give me my treasure." Elric's eyes looked crazed. "It was in my cave and you stole it from me, now return it at once."

"Your cave? I get the feeling that the cave belongs to the gnomes and not you. I think you were there stealing from them," said Stone. "Tell me I'm wrong."

"Of course, you're wrong!" This accusation seemed to anger the little man even more. "And if I say the treasure is mine, then it's mine. Now hand it over. It doesn't belong to you." Stone wasn't sure that the elf wasn't going to start steaming from the ears or stamping his foot next.

"Nope. Can't do that." Stone quickly put the rock back in his pouch. Then he reached out with an open palm just like the elf had done to him. "But you can hand over my king's wealth. Now, give it to me, and be on your way."

"I'll do no such thing." The elf hugged the bag to his chest. "You two need to go back through the portal and get out of Mura before it's too late. You don't belong here. Now leave!"

Fang growled and showed his teeth.

"And take that mangy mutt with you." The elf turned to go, but Stone didn't want him to leave yet. After all, they were in a strange land with a million unanswered questions. They needed Elric to tell them what they wanted to know and also to guide them. Hopefully, the elf would even know where to find Rancor Ruse.

"Please, wait," said Stone. "I'm looking for a man. A thief named Rancor Ruse. I want to know if you've seen him."

"The only thief I see is you!" With that, the elf dashed away, moving so fast that it was only a second before they could no longer see him.

"Well, how do you like that?" asked Aithrod. "And what do we do now? I'm tired and hungry and thirsty and need to pee."

"There must be other people around here some-where," said Stone, looking around but not seeing a soul. "I suggest we start walking and try to head for the nearest village or town." He ran a hand over the dog's head. "Fang can lead the way. Plus, I will use my tracking skills to find whoever passed through here lately."

"All right," agreed Aithrod, brushing dirt from his clothes. "And let's just hope we capture Rancor and find a way back through the portal before that irritating little elf returns."

Five

"Are you enjoying living in Mura so far?" Lira asked Persimmon the next morning. The traveling party made their way to Kascul-bough Castle, where Persimmon would be spending some time with Medea next. Rhys showed up this morning and now led the way atop his huge silver snowflake horse that was grey with white spots. The steed was like nothing she'd ever seen before. She was sure it was rare or mayhap just common here in Mura, although she didn't see another. Lira and Persimmon rode in a wagon being pulled by one normal-sized horse.

"Oh, yes, I am enjoying myself," Persimmon answered her newfound sister. "Everyone has been extremely kind and nice to me." Then she thought of the way her father had been treating her and mumbled under her breath. "Almost everyone."

Rhys escorted the women for their safety, relaying to her that they weren't far from his castle. He also told Persimmon that there were a lot of bad people who couldn't be trusted in Mura. One of those to be leery about was the evil King Sethor of Macada Castle. It was a place she had yet to see and wasn't in a hurry to visit.

"Uh oh. There seems to be a problem up ahead," Rhys called over his shoulder, stretching his neck to look down the road. "It appears to be some kind of trouble. Stay here. I'll check it out." He sped forward atop his horse, unsheathing his sword as he rode.

"What do you think is going on?" asked Persimmon. Lira pulled on the reins and stopped the horse, waiting on the road for Rhys to come back for them as ordered.

Lira shrugged. "I'm not sure. It's probably bandits."

"Bandits," Persimmon repeated, pulling her crystal orb out of her pouch. Running her hand over the smooth surface, she hoped to be able to see something that would help them. After all, her mother always used this orb to scry and help those around her when they needed guiding. Why in the world wasn't it working for her? When she looked into the orb she saw nothing. She was about to put it away when she thought she saw those same swirling colors again that she'd seen last night. But it was just a quick flash, and once again she doubted herself. Persimmon felt as if she had no power to scry and never would. A little voice in her head reminded her that she was only a half-sorceress. Perhaps that just wasn't enough power to let her see the future, and she'd only ever see a quick flash of color and nothing else.

This wasn't at all what she'd been hoping for. She sighed deeply, letting go of all hope. Then, in her mind's eye she saw two bandits attacking an older couple on the road up ahead and then running away. The thought or vision, she wasn't sure which, disappeared as fast as it came. It wasn't clear to her if it was a premonition or her imagination. Still, she felt strongly that this must have something to do with the trouble up ahead.

"Oh, nay!" she cried out, so shocked that she had finally seen something, even though it wasn't from scrying, that she almost dropped her crystal ball.

"What's the matter? What's wrong?" asked Lira in alarm, combing the area with her gaze, looking for bandits approaching.

"We must hurry. There is no time to lose." Persimmon tucked the globe back into her pouch and pulled the string closed on the velvet bag. "I think there is an old couple up ahead on the road. It must be what Rhys went to investigate. They've been robbed and beaten and will be close to dead." Persimmon grabbed the reins from Lira and urged the horse to move quickly down the road. She didn't stop until she saw Rhys. He was down on his knees leaning over the prone couple.

"We're too late," she cried, stopping the wagon and jumping off. "They were robbed and beaten and are near death," she called out to Rhys. The information spilled from her lips although she didn't really know if it was true. She ran to join him. Persimmon looked down at the victims who were an old man and old woman just like she'd seen in the vision in her mind. Falling to her knees, she used her hands to feel for pulses, shocked to see so much blood. "Oh, no. This isn't good." She shook her head. "They are severely wounded and their pulses are faint."

"I'm afraid we're too late," said Rhys. "They'll be dead before we can bring them to the castle and find help."

"Nay! Nay, we have to help them," cried Persimmon, wondering just what she could do. She didn't have the power of healing. She didn't even know how to administer the type of help that these two wounded people needed.

"What is going on here?" Lira ran up to join them, stopping in her tracks when she saw the prone, bleeding couple on the ground. She gasped.

"They need healing immediately," Rhys informed her.

"Rhys, don't you have healing powers you can use?" asked Persimmon. "After all you are half-fae, aren't you? That is what your wife told me."

"I do have the power of healing," he answered, looking sad instead of hopeful for some reason. "Unfortunately, it only works on myself. My power doesn't work on others."

"Damn," she whispered under her breath, feeling her heart go out to this old couple. Persimmon didn't like to see others suffer. She wasn't about to give up trying to help these two right now. "How about you, Lira? Is there something you can do to help them? Is there an elven power that heals?"

"Oh, sister, I wish there was, but I don't think so," she answered. "You see, my elven powers are more suitable for war, not healing. However, I do know a little about how to heal using herbs. Unfortunately, I don't have any supplies with me. Besides, that is more the skill held by the fae folk."

"Yes. We need the help of the fae," agreed Rhys.

"They will know what to do and how to heal them. Sampson, call for Murk. Quickly."

"Sampson?" Persimmon looked around them, not seeing anyone else there but them. "Who are you talking to?"

"His horse is named Sampson," Lira informed him.

"He talks to his horse?" Persimmon thought this was a little strange. "Does the horse talk back?" She wasn't trying to be snide, just honestly didn't know how things worked in Mura.

"Nay. He doesn't talk to me. Just to Murk." Rhys busied himself trying to wrap the wounds of the injured couple with some cloth he'd brought from his travel bag.

"Murk?" Why did that name sound familiar? Once again, Persimmon looked around but saw no one with them. When she turned back, Lira was pointing at the sky.

A large black raven swooped down from the air, landing on the saddle of the horse. It opened its beak and let out a few short squawks.

"Ah, Murk. Right?" Persimmon whispered to Lira, remembering hearing this bird's name mentioned at the table yesterday.

"Yes. Murk is Darium's bird," she answered.

"Murk, get Talia-Glenn," ordered Rhys. "Tell her we need her healing powers. We'll be at Kasculbough with the wounded. And tell her to hurry. They are near death."

"Wait," interrupted Lira. "Wouldn't it be better to call for your mother instead? She could get to us faster than Talia can."

"Yes. The Fae Queen will know what to do," agreed Persimmon. "Call for her. Please."

"Of course. You are right," said Rhys. "Murk, go to my mother first and then find Talia. Hurry!"

The raven shrieked and headed up into the sky.

"I'll need to get these two onto the wagon to transport them," Rhys told them.

"Do you need help moving them?" Persimmon asked him.

"Rhys has super strength," Lira informed her. "It is one of his powers."

"I see." She watched Rhys pick up the man easily, heading for the back of the wagon.

"I think I can help make things move faster." Persimmon used her power of telekinesis to assist him. Holding out her hand and focusing on what she wanted, the unconscious woman levitated and floated over to the wagon. By moving her fingers slowly, Persimmon was able to lower the old woman gently into the back of the cart.

Rhys looked up in surprise, helping to settle the old woman.

"I can move things with my mind," she explained. "I've had the ability since childhood."

"I see that," said Rhys with a nod of his head. "Thank you. Now, let's get to Kasculbough before these two die."

* * *

Stone followed Fang through a field of tall lily-type flowers, trying to find the nearest town. Even though he was a good tracker, no prints could be found. He did find a few broken stalks and knew someone had passed through the area. But this land was so clean that it even smelled beautiful. Taelgonoth stank from end to end.

Glad to be out of the cave, he had hoped the strange elf man named Elric would assist him and Aithrod, but he hadn't. It seemed as if Elric was greedy and only thought about himself. As soon as they'd exited the Quamm Caves, the elf had disappeared leaving them alone in a strange land.

"I hope we won't come across any other beings like those pesky gnomes," said Aithrod rubbing his backside as they walked.

"Or no more like that irritating, greedy little elf," added Stone.

"Mmm, these flowers smell nice." Aithrod stopped to sniff one of the lilies that was as tall as them.

"No time to stop and smell the flowers," Stone told him. "We need to keep tracking Rancor and whoever might be with him." Something made Stone stop walking to take a big sniff of one of the flowers as well. It was if the scent was starting to control his mind. Oddly enough, he started to feel randy. That's when he realized these plants must have an aphrodisiac effect on people. Something about the scent was awakening something inside him that he didn't want woke up at the moment. "Let's move faster," he said picking up the pace.

As soon as they exited the field of tall flowers, the effect thankfully wore off. They saw a small village up ahead. Colorful cottages dotted the beautiful green rolling hills. There was a creek with several arched bridges leading across the water. Blooming trees and lots and lots of lush plants and extremely large flowers covered the entire area. The air was filled with sweet smells. Butterflies and dragonflies buzzed and flitted around their heads cheerfully playing in the warm sun. Fang snapped at a butterfly and then sped across the greens chasing something that reminded Stone of a bee but was much bigger, almost the size of a bird.

"This place surely is magical," commented Aithrod. "Everything seems to be so happy and peaceful here."

"Mmmph," snorted Stone, always suspicious and never believing anything he saw. Especially when it seemed too good to be true. "Rancor and his friend could be hiding here so don't get too relaxed. We need to stay on alert at all times."

"Of course. You're right," agreed Aithrod as they crossed a bridge, trying to catch up to the hound that was running in circles in the front yard of one of the cottages.

"Fang, come back here," called out Stone. As soon as they got close to the dog, the door of the cottage opened and a woman in a flowing pink gown walked out to greet them.

"Greetings," she called out with a wave of her hand. "Are you boys lost?"

"Hello," said Aithrod, smiling and walking right up to meet her, already forgetting to remain cautious.

"We've been told we are in Mura, but that means little to us," Stone relayed the information.

"I see. I didn't think you looked familiar, even though I can't say I know everyone in Mura."

"We're from Taelgonoth and arrived here through

a portal," Aithrod blurted out, making Stone cringe. Stone wasn't sure they should be providing so much information to a stranger they'd just met. After all, it was evident that they couldn't trust the elf so why should this be any different?

"You came here through a portal? Really?" asked the kind lady, seeming very much interested in what they had to say.

"Stay quiet," Stone warned him, speaking from the side of his mouth. "We don't know if we can trust her."

"Where was this portal?" asked the woman in curiosity.

Aithrod looked over to Stone, raising his eyebrows.

Stone let out a puff of air from his mouth and shrugged. "All right, I'll tell her. It was in the cave," he said, hoping this woman would be helpful instead of a hindrance like Elric or the gnomes. "A crazy elf told us they are called the Quamm Caves."

"Oh, my. The Quamm Caves are dangerous," said the woman. "Did you have any encounters with the gnomes?"

"You could say that." Stone rubbed his behind that still hurt from being poked and pricked.

"Yes, we did. Thankfully, Elric helped us to ward them off," answered Aithrod.

"Did you say Elric?" The woman cocked her head. "What was he doing in the caves?"

"Pardon me, but we are parched and famished," said Stone, not caring to talk about the elf right now. "Would there be a chance of getting some bread and ale?"

"Silly me. Where are my manners? I haven't even introduced myself," said the woman. "I am Alaina, Queen of the Fae."

"Fae? As in fairies?" asked Stone. "I didn't think they really existed. Of course, I shouldn't be surprised since I didn't think I'd ever see anything like those gnomes either."

"Yes, fairies are the fae folk, and we do exist," Alaina told them. "Actually, I am also an elemental."

"That's nice," said Stone, not caring at the moment what being an elemental even meant. He just wanted something to eat and drink and to be on his way to track down Rancor.

"I'm Aithrod and this is Stone," Aithrod introduced them.

"And who is this?" Alaina hunkered down and pet the dog, not at all afraid of him. "So nice to meet you, Fang," she said before they could tell her the hound's name.

"How did you know my dog's name?" asked Stone suspiciously. He scanned the area, still looking for the men he tracked. "Did Elric tell you?"

"Nay, I haven't seen Elric," she answered. "Fang told me."

"What?" gasped Aithrod.

"I am a fae," she continued. "The Fae Folk all have special powers. I am able to communicate with animals. Fang tells me you are bounty hunters tracking down a dangerous man."

Stone let out a deep breath. So much for keeping cautious. "I didn't know I had to tell the hound to be discreet, too. This land surely isn't like ours at all."

"Is there magic where you come from?" asked Alaina.

"Nay, we don't have magic in Taelgonoth," Aithrod quickly answered.

Alaina stood. "I'd like to know more about you and from where you come."

Before Stone could respond, a large raven flew overhead, squawking like crazy.

"What is it, Murk? What's wrong?" asked the woman, looking up at the bird that landed atop the roof of her cottage. "Oh, no. That is horrible. Yes, go to Talia and tell her. I will leave at once."

"Excuse me," said Stone, not liking to be left out of the conversation. "What is going on?"

"I'm sorry, but I must leave you now. There are injured people who need my help. I'll just collect my bag of herbs and be on my way."

"What about our bread and ale?" Stone felt so hungry and thirsty that he couldn't think straight. He also didn't like to be ignored and left to fend for themselves in a strange land.

"Oh, yes," she said. "I'm afraid I haven't been much of a hostess. I suppose it would be better if you just came with me and got something to eat and drink there."

"Go with you? Where?" asked Stone, following her to her cottage. She went inside and picked up her bag and returned.

"To Kasculbough Castle."

"Is that nearby?" asked Aithrod. "We don't have horses to use for travel. They didn't come through the portal with us."

"Nay, the castle is not close. It is on the other side

of the Picajord Mountains." She pointed to high mountains far in the distance.

"How long does it take to get there on foot?" asked Stone.

"On foot, it would take days I imagine."

"Do you have horses we can use as well?" he asked.

"Nay, I don't have any horses. However, I have a very fast way of getting there."

"How?" asked Stone.

"I can show you. But you might want to hold on to your dog so he doesn't get scared."

"Scared? Of what?"

"I am an Elemental of the Air," she told them, but it meant nothing at all to Stone. "Hold on to your things." Alaina lifted her hands and the air started swirling all around her.

"Egads, we must be in the middle of a cyclone," said Stone, bending down to grab Fang.

"Not a cyclone. Or not exactly," stated Alaina. "I can control the air. It will give us a lift to Kascul-bough in no time at all."

"Naaay," shouted Aithrod as his feet left the ground and he shot up into the air.

"Oh, crap," mumbled Stone, holding the dog tighter. Fang whimpered and the dog's feet went wild as both Stone and Fang left the ground next, rising up into the sky. Higher and higher they went until the little cottage was nothing but a dot below them in the far distance. Stone's head spun. His stomach lurched and he felt as if he were about to vomit. "Hang in there, Fang," he told the dog. "I'm afraid this one is going to be an even harder landing than before."

Six

When Persimmon and her traveling party got to Kasculbough Castle, Medea ran out to greet them.

"Rhys? What is going on?" asked Medea, seeing the unconscious bodies in the back of the wagon. It caused a stir, bringing servants and others who lived there to wander out to see what was happening.

"Medea, I need you to get Talia and bring her back. Quickly."

"All right, but tell me more."

"These people have been robbed and attacked on the road," Persimmon interrupted. "They are near dead and need someone who can try to heal them."

"What about your mother, Rhys?" asked his wife.

"I think she's coming now." Lira pointed to the sky.

Persimmon looked up to see black clouds. The wind picked up and she saw the air spiraling in the distance. Then, to her surprise, she noticed people and even a dog flying through the sky. Since Persimmon knew the Elemental of the Air, she realized what Alaina was capable of doing. Still, she was in awe each time she witnessed it.

"I will be right back." Medea disappeared into thin air, doing her little transporting thing.

"Let's get the injured inside," suggested Rhys, dismounting his horse.

"I'll take care of the woman," offered Persimmon, but by the time she could get off the bench seat of the wagon, Rhys had the man in one arm and the woman in his other arm and was hurrying toward the castle. The onlookers started to crowd around.

"I'll fetch some rags and water." Lira was off at a run. Persimmon was about to follow her when she heard shouting from above her.

"Watch out!" someone screamed.

She looked up to see a man falling fast—right toward her.

"Nay!" She raised her hands to block her head, not wanting to get hurt. That's when she felt the impact of him as his body crashed into hers. Both of them fell to the ground and she heard a clattering sound like wood hitting stone from behind them.

"Ooomph!" The air was knocked from her lungs as the man landed directly on top of her. Both of them lay spread out in the courtyard in a very compromising position.

The servants and nobles all gathered around curiously as Alaina landed gently without even making a sound. Another man fell to the cobbled stones after that, and a dog landed atop him.

"I'm sorry," said the man on top of Persimmon,

hurrying to get to his feet. "I didn't mean for this to happen. I hope I didn't hurt you."

"I'm all right."

"I'm not used to this way of traveling and don't know how to land." He reached for her hand to help her get up off the ground.

"I didn't expect to get hit by a man falling from the sky today." Persimmon, being pulled to a standing position, looked up to see one of the most handsome men she'd ever laid eyes on in her life. A rugged man with shoulder-length ebony hair perused her with steely gray eyes that held the intensity of a hawk. He stood tall, towering over her. His wide shoulders tapered down to a trim waist. He was dressed in traveling clothes, and also wore a cloak. Flung over one of his shoulders was a crossbow, which made her wonder if perhaps he was a hunter. However, he had a sword at his side, too, making her believe he was more of a fighting man. A smattering of peppered stubble covered his sculpted jaw. He looked sincerely sorry, as well as terribly tired.

"It's all right," she said flashing him a smile. "No harm done. I hope," she added, her hands searching out her pouch to check on her gazing orb. If it was smashed, she would be so upset. This was all she had left to remember her mother. "Oh, good. It's all right." She breathed a sigh of relief, pulling out the orb and holding it in two hands up to her chest. When she did, she suddenly she saw a flash of a vision in her mind again. This time it was the man who stood in front of her right now. And he was kissing her. "Oh, my!"

"What is that?" He looked at her curiously, the side of his mouth curving up into a half-smile.

"It's...it's nothing." Feeling a blush of embarrassment rise to her cheeks, hoping he wasn't able to read her mind, she quickly slipped the glass ball back into her pouch.

"Wow, was that an exciting yet terrifying ride. I never want to do it again." The other man walked over to them, brushing off his clothes. A dog followed him over. "Oh, who is this?"

"I'm Persimmon Burroughs," she introduced herself. "Who are you two?"

"I'm Aithrod Gabbencort and—"

The man's friend cut him off. "I am Stone Nightstalker and this is my dog, Fang. Nice to meet you. Although, I wish our meeting could have been a bit more...subtle shall we say?"

"Persimmon, where is my son?" asked Alaina. "Murk told me there are injured people who need my help."

"They are in the keep, my Queen," Persimmon told her. "Let me take you to them." She glanced back at the handsome man, wanting one more look before she walked away. "Would you care to join us inside the castle?"

"Is there food and drink in there?" he asked instead of answering her directly.

"I'm sure there is. After all, this is a castle. I am sure they'll have the richest food and the most bountiful drinks fit for a king."

"Then what are we waiting for?" Stone bent down and picked up a long staff that must have fallen with him from the sky.

Persimmon watched him, surprised she hadn't even noticed the staff. Now, she realized what made the noise she had heard when he fell from the sky.

"Are you a hunter?" she asked, as he, his friend, and the dog followed her to the keep.

"In a way I guess I am a hunter," Stone answered.

"He's a bounty hunter," Aithrod told her, correcting any idea of him she had in her head.

"You are?" She stopped and looked him up and down. "So, you hunt men, not animals." The idea disgusted her and she didn't quite know what to think.

Stone could tell by the look on the girl's face that she wasn't pleased at hearing about his profession. There was an accusing look in her bright blue eyes that suddenly made him feel as if he had done something wrong. Her endearing smile disappeared fast. Now her full pink lips turned down into a half-frown.

"I bring in criminals so justice can be served," he tried to explain to her. "Is there something wrong with that?"

"I don't feel as if anyone deserves to be put behind bars or executed."

"Really?" He raised a brow. "If you truly believe that, then you must be living a very sheltered life, my dear. The guilty need to be punished for hurting the good. If you were in my land, you'd see how badly it has deteriorated because of this exact thing. I am trying to bring it back to where it should be, a safe place to live."

"Your land?" she asked. "Where is that?"

Stone let out a deep breath and answered at the same time as Aithrod.

"Taelgonoth."

The girl cocked her pretty little head, appearing quite confused.

"I am not familiar with Taelgonoth. Is your home far from here?" she asked them.

"I suppose it depends on how you travel," Stone said with a chuckle, thinking about the way they'd just got here from the other side of the mountain in mere minutes.

"We came through a portal," explained Aithrod. "We're not exactly sure about time."

"A portal?" she asked. Her eyes darted around and she held a finger to her lips. "Shhh. Don't even say that word around here. I was warned not to."

"You were?" asked Stone in confusion. "Why?"

Stone didn't miss the fact her eyes darted down to the pouch hanging at her side. She was looking to that crystal sphere in the velvet bag again. Portals also seemed to interest her, although she didn't seem willing to speak about them aloud for some odd reason. Something also told him that she was another of these magical beings who lived in this odd land called Mura.

"I believe they brought the injured to the solar," Persimmon told Alaina. "I will join you."

"Nay, it'll be fine." Alaina looked over at the men and dog. "Persimmon, will you please do me a favor and see to our guests? I promised them food and drink."

"She is a guest here as well, my Queen." A girl

with strawberry-blonde hair hurried out of the kitchen with several servants following her. They held rags and bowls of hot water.

"Lira, this is Stone and Aithrod. And Fang," Persimmon introduced them.

"Hello," said the girl named Lira with a nod. She smiled, but worry darkened her face. "I can help your men."

"Nay, it's fine," said Persimmon. "I don't mind doing it. Besides, it would be beneficial for you to stay with the wounded. I will find the kitchen on my own and get these men something to eat and drink."

"Thank you, sister." Lira hurried off with the others to help the injured.

"She's your sister?" asked Stone, noticing that the girl who just left them had pointy ears and Persimmon didn't. Plus, one had light hair and the other was stark black.

"Yes, Lira is my sister, but I just found that out. This way," she told them, leading them to the kitchen.

"You didn't know you had a sister?" Stone thought this sounded odd. Especially since they were both in their twenties already.

"Nay," she told Stone. "My father never mentioned it to me. She is my half-sister, actually. We both share the same father. I came here to Mura to find him since my mother just died. Sadly, my father doesn't seem to want me."

"That's horrible," said Stone, reaching down to pet his dog on the head as they walked. "I'm sorry to say that your father seems like quite a—"

"Quite a what, you big oaf?"

Stone stopped when the elf they'd seen in the caves suddenly appeared standing in front of him. Stone almost crashed right into him. Elric had his hands on his hips again, and as he'd already learned, that wasn't a good thing. The dog growled lowly at seeing the elf, and Aithrod groaned.

"What are you doing here?" asked Stone. "I thought you abandoned us."

"Stone, this is my father, Elric." Persimmon held out a hand to introduce them. "And, yes, Father, why are you here?"

"Talk about not being wanted, I feel as if none of you want me here. Therefore, I'll just leave." Elric made a haughty face.

"Nay, wait!" Stone held up a halting hand to stop him. "I want to talk to you."

"If it's about—" Elric stopped and glanced over to his daughter before saying more. "If it's about anything we've already discussed, forget it. You're not getting anything from me."

"Father, what are you talking about?" asked Persimmon.

"Nothing," said Elric, picking invisible lint from his tunic.

"By nothing, he means the gemstones he found in the Quamm Caves. Gems that were stolen from our king on Taelgonoth." Stone glared at the little man.

"I didn't steal anything, and I won't stand here being accused of crimes I didn't commit." Elric's chin lifted up into the air. "I told you before, I found them."

"Father, do they mean stones like the one you

were using as part of your bid in your card game when I arrived?" asked Persimmon.

"You did what?" Stone was aghast at hearing this. How could anyone take such a risk with such a valuable item?

"You're not helping matters, daughter," grumbled the little man. "And you wonder why I favor Lira over you. I have things to do. I need to go." In a blur, the elf was gone.

Stone looked up to see the wetness of Persimmon's eyes. Her father had been harsh with her. It hurt him to see anyone treat this kind woman so badly.

"Don't let him upset you with his crass words." Stone stepped forward and took her by the arm. "Let's find some food and ale. Then we can all sit down and talk. I'd like to hear all about you, Persimmon Burroughs. You seem like such a fascinating young woman."

"I don't think my father would agree with you on that." Her words sounded as if they held shame.

"I get the feeling your father wouldn't agree with anyone if his life depended on it," Stone responded. "But I am, I assure you, much more of a benevolent man than Elric in any land."

That made her smile. It was good to see the spark of light and hope return to her eyes.

"Yes. Yes, I believe you are," she told him, using the back of her hand to wipe away a stray tear from her cheek. "Now, let's get you two some food and ale and go back out to the great hall so we can get to know each other."

The dog sat down and whined. His tail swept back and forth over the floor.

"I'm sure I can find something for you, too, Fang," she said with a giggle, petting the dog's nose.

"I appreciate everything, Persimmon. However, what I want even more than food or ale is information," Stone told her.

"Information?" She looked up at him and her brows angled. "What do you mean?"

"Well, first of all, I need to collect those gemstones from your father. Then I need to find a different thief and his counterpart and get back through the portal and return the stolen gems to our king. Therefore, I'll need to know where Elric lives."

"Oh." Her smile was gone, and she suddenly became guarded. "I can't help you because I don't know where to find Elric. I have no idea where he lives."

"You don't know where your own father lives?" asked Aithrod. "How can you not?"

"It's the truth," she said, looking upset that they didn't believe her. "Now, let us get that food so you men and poor little Fang don't starve to death."

Persimmon could tell by the look on Stone's face that he didn't believe her at all when she said she didn't know where her father lived. She supposed it wasn't quite the truth. Since being here in Mura she heard that her sister, Lira banished Elric to some high cliff in Glint to live by himself. Still, she had never been there personally and couldn't give anyone directions. Persimmon had never even been to the elven land of Glint before, but heard it was on the other side of the

Picajord Mountains. The land of the elves actually sounded exciting to her. It was a place that she would very much like to visit someday to find out about the elven race and understand more about herself.

It was a new feeling for her, but part of Persimmon didn't want Stone to ever know where to find Elric. She supposed it was because if he knew, there was a good chance he'd collect his king's gemstones and head back through the portal and she would never see him again. After having glimpsed an image in her mind of them kissing, she selfishly wanted time for that to come true.

Persimmon's life had been sad, quiet and lonely. To her, that was true imprisonment. She was the type of person who loved being around people. She liked conversing with men as well. Living most of her life in a convent, she was never allowed to have a normal life, and still wondered why her mother put her there. All her mother ever told her about it was that Persimmon would be protected there. From who or what was information that had never been divulged to her.

Persimmon found herself intrigued by Stone Nightstalker, even if she didn't like the fact he hunted men for a living even if they were bad. He said he wanted to know all about her, but she wanted parts of her past life to stay hidden. Nay, she didn't want to tell him much about her childhood because it brought up sad feelings in her heart. She was done being sad. Here on Mura she had a new life to look forward to, and here is where she could be happy for the rest of her life.

Deciding she would have to conceive a plan that would keep Stone here for a while until they got closer, she would need to do the only thing she could think of that might work. Still having the vision of them kissing burned into her mind, she realized she was going to either have to tell him about it, or kiss him herself, to make him want to stay.

Persimmon sat at one of the long trestle tables in the great hall with Stone and his friend. She was too nervous around Stone to eat, and held her goblet of wine with two hands. She had never had the attention of a handsome man before. She wasn't even used to being so close to one and this was pleasing.

"Here you go, Fang." Stone bent over and gave a good part of his food to the dog. Fang sat under the table at his feet, begging.

"I asked one of the servants to bring a bone for your dog as well," she told him.

"Thank you." Stone picked up his goblet, taking a drink and looking at her with those intense grey eyes over the rim of his cup. His friend, Aithrod didn't even look up as he hungrily devoured his food.

"I'd like to know more about the—the portal," she said, whispering the last word, not wanting to upset anyone since Zann warned her not to talk about it. She lifted her goblet and drank as well, staring right back at him. Something about his gaze seemed to make her heart race faster as well as her body to heat up at the same time. It didn't make sense at all.

"We don't know anything about the portal," said Aithrod, picking up a baked chicken leg and taking a big bite.

"That's right," Stone said, slowly putting down his goblet. "We saw a portal and walked through it and ended up here in Mura. That's about it."

"And you're looking for a thief," she added.

"Actually, three thieves now. Two from my land, and the one from yours," he continued.

"You mean my father." She picked up the goblet and drank again.

"Yes. Rancor Ruse, we believe has another man with him from Taelgonoth. We need to find them and the king's jewels and bring the thieves back to King Helix so they can be properly punished."

"What about my father?" she asked. "Do you plan to bring him back to your king to be punished or executed as well?"

"I'm...not sure." Stone popped a piece of cooked carrot into his mouth and chewed. "Elric is a thief and cannot get away with taking the king's jewels. I won't allow it."

"How could he have gone through a portal to steal them? That is absurd to even think that."

"Elric said he found the gems in the cave, but we don't believe him," Aithrod told her between bites.

"Yes, he did tell us that," said Stone. "Then again, he also claimed the cave was his, so what does that tell you?"

"I don't know," she answered. "What does it tell you?"

"It tells me that he is either a liar, or if he really did find the stones in the cave, that means Rancor dropped them which is highly unlikely."

"Mayhap Rancor dropped them when he was trying to fend off those pesky gnomes." Aithrod bit into a crunchy apple.

"I suppose that could be true," said Stone. "Or another possibility is that your father stole them from Rancor when he came through the portal and zipped away before anyone could stop him. We've all seen how fast he can move."

"Yes, he does move fast," Persimmon agreed. She wanted to defend her father, but she honestly didn't trust him any more than Stone did, so she said nothing.

"Here is the bone for the dog," said a servant boy holding it out to Persimmon.

"Thank you." Stone snatched it up and gave it to the dog under the table. Fang laid down, holding the bone between his paws and eagerly gnawing at it.

"Persimmon, come quickly." Lira ran up to the table. "The old couple cannot be healed. It looks as if they will die. We need you."

"Oh, no," said Persimmon, getting to her feet. "Lira, what can I do? I can't heal. You know that."

"I do. But you have your crystal ball. Mayhap you can look into it and tell us what needs to be done."

"What?" Her heart lodged in her throat. They were counting on her to help them, thinking she could really scry. Oh, why hadn't she corrected the misunderstanding when it first happened? It was going to be so hard to do so now when they were all counting on her. "Nay, Lira. I don't think so." How could she admit to the others that she had never seen anything in the gazing orb besides quick flashes of swirling colors? Her new friends wouldn't trust her if they knew. And her father would only hate her even more. Oh, what a mess she was in.

"Don't be silly. Of course, she'll do it." Stone pushed away his plate and stood. "Aithrod, watch over Fang. I'm going, too." He took Persimmon by the arm and started walking.

"No, wait," she tried to protest, but Stone didn't let her back out. He was holding her arm tightly and she had no choice but to go along with them.

"The solar is just through here." Lira led the way.

"I told you, I cannot help." Persimmon didn't like this. She tried to squirm out of Stone's hold, but he wouldn't let her loose.

"Cannot or will not?" asked Stone as they continued to walk. "It seems to me you have powers that could be helpful but for some reason are not inclined to use them on those who need them. You are being selfish. Much like your father."

"Nay, I'm not. You don't understand. It's not true!"

"Then prove it," he challenged her as they reached the solar door. "Use your gazing crystal to see what these fae folk can do to ensure that this elderly couple will not die."

"It isn't as easy as you think," she protested as Stone opened the door and gently pushed her into the room.

Persimmon stopped in her tracks when she entered the room to find both the old man and old woman standing at the foot of the bed dressed all in white. That would have been a miraculous recovery if they were well enough to stand. However, it wasn't so. She realized that as soon as she saw the old couple peering down at themselves on the bed. It was happening again, even if she didn't want it to. She was seeing ghosts, or spirits. This is something that started happening to her and it frightened her to no end. She didn't want to see ghosts. She usually closed her eyes and told them to leave, but she couldn't do that right now.

One of the main reasons she left Lornoon in the first place was because she kept seeing the ghost of her dead mother and it scared her out of her wits. She thought if she'd come here to find her father, the ghostly apparition would stay in Lornoon. Now it looked like other ghosts had found her here.

"What's the matter?" asked Stone. "You look like you're about to faint."

"I...I...nothing." She looked away from the ghosts, not wanting to see them, willing the images to fade from her sight.

"Sister, please. Help us," begged Lira. "We no longer know what to do. Even with Alaina's ministrations and also Talia's, I fear it might be too late for these poor people."

Persimmon looked over at the bed to see that Darium's wife Talia had arrived as well. Darium stood in the shadows, silently watching.

"Go on. Get your gazing orb out." Stone tapped the pouch at her side.

Not knowing what to do, Persimmon slowly reached for her gazing orb, sliding it out of her pouch.

Nervously, she once more glanced up at the ghosts that only she could see.

We are near dead. This came from the ghost of the man. He spoke to her in her mind and Persimmon still couldn't accept that she was really hearing him.

Tell her about the men who did this to us, said his wife. *Tell her so they can catch them.*

"Persimmon? What are you waiting for?" Stone dragged her from her thoughts.

"Huh?" Her head snapped around to see him staring down at her.

"What's wrong? You look so pale and frightened. Almost as if you've seen a ghost," he continued.

"Nay! Why would you even say that?" Her gaze flitted back over to the old couple again. Their images were fading in and out.

There were two men, said the old woman. *They both had dark hair and beards.*

They accused us of stealing some of their stones, but we don't know why they said that, added the man. *When we said we didn't have them or even know what they were talking about, they robbed us and tried to kill us.*

They weren't from Mura. They looked different, said the woman. *I am sure I've never seen them here before.*

"Sister, are you coming?" Lira called to her from the bedside. "Please, hurry. It's important. Their lives depend on it."

"The herbs didn't work." Alaina hovered over the couple, feeling for pulses.

"They lost too much blood," said Talia. "I'm afraid they're going to die."

"Yes," said Persimmon, pretending to look into her crystal ball. "They are. There is nothing we can do to save them. I'm sorry." She quickly replaced the gazing ball in the bag.

Fast, ask her, the old woman said to her husband.

We want the Sin Eater to tend to us once we pass away, said the old man. *We don't want to go to The Dark Abyss since we never had time to confess our sins.*

"I wish we could do something for them," said Alaina. "I tried everything, but it isn't working."

"What about the Elemental, Portia-Maer? The one with the healing kiss." Darium stepped forward, looking down at the couple and shaking his head. "Couldn't she help them?"

"Yes, she probably could," said Alaina. "However, it is not right to ask my friend to use her healing powers every time someone is dying. If so, no one would ever die, and that would be a problem. It is part of the cycle of nature to die. Mayhap it is this couple's destiny to go this way."

"I no longer believe we have destinies, but that we make our own," said Darium with a shake of his head. "But I suppose I understand what you are saying. Well, there is nothing more any of us can do then. I will take care of burying their bodies as soon as they cross over."

Ask him! Quickly, said the man, looking directly at Persimmon.

"I don't understand what you mean," she whispered to the ghost man, but Stone heard her.

"Who are you talking to?" he asked, looking around. "And what don't you understand?"

"I will make the proper preparations and notify the gravedigger." Darium started for the door.

"Sin Eater," she repeated the words aloud, still puzzled by what they meant. Darium stopped in his tracks. His head slowly turned and his blue eyes fixated on her.

"What did you say?" he asked in a deep voice, making her feel as if she'd somehow said something wrong.

Go on. Ask him. He's the one. The old couple huddled together, looking so lost and forlorn. She had to try to help them somehow even if she wasn't able to save their lives.

"They'll need a sin eater," she said, dropping her gaze to the ground and swallowing deeply.

"What the hell is a Sin Eater?" asked Stone, seeming amused by the words.

"I—I'm not sure," she whispered, staring at the floor now and wringing her hands together.

"I am a Sin Eater." Darium turned and scrutinized Stone now. "Or, should I say I used to be."

"Oh." Stone's smiled disappeared. "So, it is a real thing then?"

"My husband doesn't sin eat anymore, I'm sorry." Talia hurried over to join them.

Please. Don't let us go to The Dark Abyss, begged the old woman, but, of course, Persimmon was the only one who could hear or see the ghosts.

"He has to," said Persimmon. "If not, the couple might go to The Great Abyss?" She wasn't sure what any of this meant. They didn't speak this way on

Lornoon. She just repeated the message, hoping someone would understand.

"The Great Abyss? What is that?" asked Stone.

"It's a place that no one ever wants to go. And that means me, too," answered Darium.

"I don't understand," said Persimmon. "What does this all mean?"

"My husband used to be a Sin Eater, taking on the sins of others at death," explained Talia. "However, by doing this, in exchange, it condemned him to spend eternity in The Dark Abyss instead."

"The Dark Abyss is what some people call Hell," explained Darium, seeing that she and Stone didn't understand.

"He eats...sins?" Stone ran a hand through his long hair, looking like he couldn't believe it.

"Yes. Food and drink is placed atop the chests of the dead who died before they were able to confess their sins," Darium explained. "I absorb their sins by eating and drinking the items from their bodies."

"I have never heard anything so absurd," said Stone. "You are not really going to do it?"

"Is that what you saw in the crystal orb?" asked Darium. "Is that what I'm to do?"

"Well I...yes, it is." Persimmon answered, not wanting the old couple to go to such a dark place for all eternity. She also didn't want to explain about her lack of power with the crystal orb or the fact she could see ghosts. She wasn't sure how others would view her if they knew the truth.

"But you weren't even looking into the gazing orb when you told us that," said Stone softly, but thankfully no one else heard him.

"Even if that is what the prophetess saw, you shouldn't do it, Darium," warned Talia. "Please, don't risk it again."

"Remember, I make my own destiny now, Talia." Darium told his wife. "Besides, I was given a healing kiss by the Elemental of the Air, Portia-Maer. She said, even if I did sin eat from now on it would be my choice. She told me I won't take on the darkness of others anymore, either way."

"There is no one here that knows this couple to mourn them or to ask you to sin eat for them," Talia pointed out. "I don't see the purpose in it."

"That's true," agreed Lira. "You usually do it to help the living of the deceased find solace. This couple have no one that we know of. It's not necessary."

We have a son, said the man.

His name is Gregor, added the woman. *Gregor Lithum. He needs to know. Please find him and tell him what happened.*

Persimmon quickly pulled the orb back out and held it in two hands before she spoke. "They have a son and they want us to find him," she told the others, seeing the sadness on the couple's faces.

"Really. What else do you see in the gazing crystal?" asked Stone, sounding suspicious of her. "And why aren't you even looking at it?"

Persimmon closed her eyes and released a deep breath. "It is important to the elderly couple that their son comes to them now."

"Ask the gazing orb where we can find their son," said Darium.

The woman answered, having heard the question. *Our son resides at Macada Castle.*

Gregor works for King Sethor, although we don't agree with it. We haven't spoken with him for years, added the man.

"I know his name and where to find him." Persimmon quickly put away her gazing ball once more before Stone could point out again to everyone that she wasn't even looking into it.

"Great," said Darium. "So tell me, and I will go and fetch him. Where can I find their son?"

"His name is Gregor Lithum and he resides at Macada Castle," she told the others.

"Oh, crap," Darium said under his breath. "Anywhere but there."

"What's the matter?" asked Stone.

"That is where the evil King Sethor resides. He is the enemy of all the magical beings of Mura," Darium explained.

"You can't go there, Darium. Please," begged his wife, trying to stop him.

"It seems important to this dying couple. We must do it. For their sakes. It will be fine," Darium told his wife, giving her a hug.

"It sounds like the exact place where a thief would hide." Stone nodded and rubbed his chin in thought. "Yes, it is. I will go with you to Macada Castle, Darium, because I am tracking two men from Taelgonoth that I believe could be hiding there. And I am sure Aithrod will want to join us, too."

You need to go as well, the old woman told Persimmon, but Persimmon pretended not to hear her.

They might not be able to find Gregor. We can guide you to him, said the man.

Please. He is all we have left in this world. The woman clung to her husband, looking as if she were about to cry.

"I guess I'll go, too," Persimmon blurted out before she could change her mind.

"Sister, nay. It is too dangerous," warned Lira. "Stay here at Kasculbough where you'll be safe."

Persimmon struggled with her decision, but realized both Darium and Stone were doing what they believed was for the best. She had done nothing to help save this couple's lives, but mayhap she could help bring about justice for their senseless deaths if they perished.

"It is my decision, and I want to go, too," said Persimmon with conviction.

"Then what are we waiting for?" Darium led the way out the door. "I will take Murk with us and send him back with word on what is transpiring. He'll let the rest of you know if we should happen to encounter trouble."

"Persimmon? Are you ready?" Stone's hand was on her arm again. She flashed him a smile and headed out the door, hoping that after this she would never have to see a ghost or a spirit or be asked to scry using her crystal ball ever again.

Eight

"Come on, Fang," Stone called to his dog as he mounted a horse that King Rhys had offered.

"I should come along with you," said Rhys. "My strength might come in handy."

"Nay, Brother, that's not a good idea." Darium mounted a horse as well. "There are already too many of us in this traveling party. Your presence as King of Kasculbaugh will only put Sethor on defense. If he sees you, he'll order an attack before he even knows why we are there. I am not as big of a threat to him as you are. I have also done sin eating for him before, so hopefully he'll trust me enough to at least let me in the gate and listen to why we are there. So you see, I am the one who needs to go."

"We'll tell him he might have a thief hiding inside his walls," said Aithrod from atop his horse. "Any king would be anxious to catch such a person."

"Not this one," said Darium in a low voice. "Knowing King Leofric Sethor, he'd probably side with the thief you are searching for. I wouldn't doubt your hunted man will be convinced to do the king's bidding while he is here in Mura."

Stone saw Persimmon just standing there, doing nothing to prepare for the journey. "Please hurry, Persimmon," urged Stone. "Mount your steed. We need to leave at once. Time is of the essence."

Persimmon stood there staring at the horse, not even touching it. Then her body stiffened. "I can't," she said from the ground, making Stone believe she had changed her mind about going along with them.

"That's fine. I understand, if you changed your mind and don't want to go. It's all right," he told her. "You can stay here where you're safe. It's better that way."

"Nay, I do want to come with you. That's not what I mean at all."

"Then what is it?" asked Stone. "I don't understand."

The girl shifted from foot to foot, seeming very uncomfortable.

"I can't ride," she finally mumbled.

"Oh, you want a lady's saddle?" asked Rhys who was there to see them off. "I can arrange that. My wife likes to ride astride so I'm just used to saddling all the horses that way." He raised his hand to call over the stable boy, but Persimmon stopped him.

"Nay, please, don't bother. The saddle won't help," she told him. "I have never ridden a horse before and I'm not even sure I can do it."

"What?" Stone laughed, thinking at first she was jesting. But when he saw the tears in her eyes, he realized she was being serious. "Oh, you really can't ride," he said, clearing his throat. He had never heard of anyone who was as old as she who had never been atop a horse before. It seemed ridiculous to him. Then again, he was in a strange land now. He wasn't sure if sorceresses, or whatever she was, could even do such things.

"You'd better stay here then," suggested Darium.

"Nay. I need to accompany you. The old couple insisted I go to find their son," protested Persimmon.

"They insisted?" asked Stone. "How? Through the gazing ball?"

"It doesn't matter how I know," she said, her voice cracking. "All I can tell you is that it is very important that I accompany you on this journey."

Stone could see the turmoil on the girl's face. He could tell it was really important to her to do as the dying couple wished. Or what she thought they wished, anyway. Stone wasn't sure he was buying any of this about the girl being able to see the future or talk to dying people through that damned ball. Then again, if not, he wasn't sure why Persimmon would make up something like this that could actually get her killed. However, joining them on the trip to Macada Castle didn't seem to terrify her half as much as the thought of getting on a horse.

"She can ride with me," he told the others, reaching down for the girl. "Grab on, and I'll pull you up."

"I'm not sure," she said, being hesitant to take his hand. Stone didn't give her a chance to object. He grabbed on to her and lifted her up in front of him atop the horse, wrapping his arms around her waist, still holding the reins. Fang barked and ran in circles below them. "We're ready," he told the others with a nod. "Let's go catch our thieves."

If Persimmon wasn't already nervous enough being atop a horse, now she was feeling even more uncomfortable sitting with her back pressed up against the handsome stranger's chest. Stone also had his arms around her waist. Never before had she been so close to a man that they were actually touching. She could feel his body heat against her back. His scent of leather, the outdoors, and woodsmoke filled her senses, oddly bringing her to life. Persimmon had led a very sheltered life living at the convent, and never before had she been as intimate with a man as she was at this very moment.

"Relax, I'm not going to hurt you," came his voice in her ear. His cheek was pressed up against the side of her head. When he spoke she could feel the vibration of his deep voice rumbling in his chest. His breath whisked past her ear, causing a delicious shiver to spiral through her.

"I am relaxed," she told him, not wanting him to know how affected she was by just being in his presence.

"Your back is as straight as a rod and even your words are stiff and forced," he replied. "What is it about me that makes you so nervous?"

The man was very observant, she'd give him that. She supposed it was part of his training to be observant, being a bounty hunter. "It's not you making me nervous," she told him, even though he made her knees quake. "You see, when I was a young girl I was thrown from a horse and almost died. I haven't been riding since." This was the truth. She had been just a child at the time. It had happened right before her mother sent her to live at the convent. Since the nuns didn't ride horses, she never had the opportunity to get atop a horse again, only making her fearful memories stronger.

"Didn't your mother make you get right back on the horse?" he asked.

"Nay. My mother didn't spend a lot of time with me when I was growing up."

"You are different from the other women here," he said his thought aloud.

"It's because I am a stranger to this land," she reminded him. "I have never been anywhere besides Lornoon. I admit, I know very little about the land of Mura or its people."

"The same goes for me," he replied. "I am a stranger here, too." She shifted atop the horse, trying to make space between them. "Does that worry you?"

"I don't know you at all so I am not sure what to think about you quite yet," is all she said, having learned to always be cautious and to trust no one. Still, she felt protected in his embrace and that couldn't be a bad thing.

"I'd like to change that, Persimmon. Mayhap you can tell me a little more about yourself and the land you come from."

They continued to ride. Aithrod talked with

Darium who was leading the way. Fang was up front as well. Stone and Persimmon brought up the rear.

"I'd rather you told me about yourself and where you come from instead," she said, not wanting to talk about herself since she felt she was naught but a boring girl.

"All right," he agreed. "I am Stone Nightstalker as you already know. I come from a land called Taelgonoth. I cannot tell you where it is from here since we came through a portal and I am not sure how we got here."

"Yes. So, you've said."

"What else do you want to know?"

"Are you married? Do you have children?" She looked up from the side of her eye, waiting for him to answer, hoping he didn't have someone back home waiting for him.

"Nay to both. How about you?"

She let out the breath she hadn't realized she'd been holding. "Me? Married?" She couldn't help but smile. "No, I'm not married and I don't have children."

"That seemed to amuse you," said Stone.

"No one has ever asked me that question before."

"Why not? A beautiful woman like you back on Taelgonoth would have been married for years and have at least a half dozen children by now."

"Really?" She turned and looked over her shoulder at him which only made their faces even closer. Mayhap she shouldn't have done that. It seemed to be such an intimate move. "Are all the women in Taelgonoth beautiful?" she asked, needing to know.

"I think every woman, no matter where she comes from, has beauty in one way or another," he answered. "But you, my lady, are by far the prettiest one I have ever met."

"Oh!" That took her by surprise. No one had ever called her beautiful before. "Please, don't use a title when you refer to me. I am not a lady," she pointed out.

"Well, your father is also father to Queen Lira, so doesn't that make you a noble, too?" he asked, which made sense. "Or at least a half-royal?"

"I believe Lira's mother was the royal one, not our father," she said, as the thought caught her off guard. "I have only just found out I have a queen sister, so I have never thought about that before.

"Speaking of your father, tell me something. Why doesn't the elf seem to like you? It strikes me as odd. I mean, you are his daughter."

"I really couldn't tell you the answer to that." Persimmon longed for the attention of Elric, especially since her mother had passed away and she had no other living relatives that she knew of. Except Lira and her brothers, as she'd just found out after getting here. "It is almost as if he despises me, but I don't know why or what I could have done to turn him against me."

"Mayhap you frighten him," said Stone.

She smiled again. "I don't think so. I'm not a very frightening person, am I?"

"Not to me, you're not," he told her. "However, you do have magical powers and mayhap it has something to do with that. Why he avoids you, I mean."

"My father has powers of his own, so I think naught."

"I see."

"Stone, I have to admit to you that I am not as powerful as you might believe."

"You are the daughter of a sorceress and an elven sage. I'd say you are very powerful indeed, sweetheart."

"If so, I don't know much about my powers."

"Didn't your mother ever teach you about them?" asked Stone. "Or isn't that how it works? Since we don't have magic on Taelgonoth, I'm not certain I understand it."

"I can move objects with my mind alone," she blurted out, not even sure why she was telling him this. Since she'd just met the man, she wasn't even sure she could trust him. Still, a part of her wanted to talk to someone about this. She couldn't dismiss the fact that she wanted to say something to make him like her or respect her. Mayhap this was wrong. She no longer knew. "I have had the ability ever since I can remember. No one taught it to me. It just came naturally."

"You move objects with you mind," he repeated. "Well, that sounds pretty impressive to me. Plus, you can talk to spirits and see the future using that crystal ball of yours. Right?"

It was almost as if he were testing her. Or setting her up to catch her in a lie.

The horse stumbled a little, and he gripped her tighter in his embrace to keep her safe. "Steady, girl," he said, talking to the horse, but at the same time it was like a little voice in her ear warning her not to open up her life to this stranger too fast.

She wanted to tell him that she'd had her mother's crystal ball for a month now and it wasn't until she got to Mura that she'd ever even seen anything in it at all. Then, she decided not to divulge that information just yet. She wanted to appear to him to be a strong woman, like Medea or Alaina or Lira. Like women who impressed her and whom she respected. Sadly, she didn't feel strong in any sense, but didn't want to be viewed as weak or naive. Not answering his question, she remained silent as they rode.

"Whoa," she heard Darium from up ahead.

The travelers stopped and waited for Stone and her to join them. Fang panted and wagged his tail, almost looking as if he were smiling. The castle before them was majestic, fortified and made of stone. Thick walls made it look like it was an impenetrable fortress that no one would ever be able to escape. It sat high on a cliff overlooking the water. Flags fluttered in the breeze from the tall turrets at each corner of the citadel. It was an amazing yet at the same time a terrifying sight.

"The gate is down, so they are already wary or know we are coming," Darium announced to the others. "We'll go up the drawbridge on foot, walking our horses." He held out one leather-clad arm. His raven flew down from the sky and landed atop it. "We'll seem less threatening that way."

"Good idea." Stone slid down from the horse, holding out his arms to help her dismount.

"Thank you," she said, putting her hands on his

shoulders as he lifted her from the steed. His shoulders felt strong and sturdy under her fingers. His grip was secure yet not overwhelmingly tight. He set her on her feet, and for a brief moment their eyes interlocked. Everyone else faded away as she gazed into his steely orbs, feeling as if she could see all the way to his soul. At first, she sensed nothing but curiosity about her in his eyes. But then in the reflection of his orbs she saw something that frightened her immensely. A battle. Capture. And imprisonment. She gasped, never having seen a vision in someone's eyes before! This went far beyond what she saw in her mind or even scrying with the gazing crystal, if she had been able to use it.

"Is something wrong?" Stone asked her.

"I'm not sure." Fear coursed through her for more reasons than one. She worried for their safety, but at the same time doubted that she'd truly seen the future in the reflection of a man's eyes. How could she? This must be a new power. One which she had no idea how to control.

"We need to keep on our toes," warned Darium. "I'm not sure if we'll be welcome here."

"Once we're inside the castle walls, I'll search for Rancor and his counterpart," offered Aithrod.

"Fang can pick up his scent. Keep him at your side," said Stone.

"What about you?" asked Aithrod. "Won't you be searching for Rancor with me?"

When Stone glanced over at Persimmon, this time she saw a sadness within his eyes that she couldn't explain.

"Nay. I'll stay with Persimmon and help her find Gregor instead."

"But you're the bounty hunter, Stone. It's your job to find the thief," she told him.

"I feel my job is to protect you now, and that is what I've decided to do." Stone sounded firm with his decision. "I am not leaving your side while we are here, sweetheart."

"Thank you," she whispered, feeling choked up that this man who was naught but a stranger to her would put her safety over the importance of a job he needed to do for his king. She wasn't sure why he had decided this, but figured she would ask him about it later. Right now, she was basking in the fact that he had just called her sweetheart. Again. It made her feel important. Special. Pretty. These were things she had never felt before now.

"I will try to keep King Sethor busy and also from killing us." Darium adjusted the sword on his back.

"Won't we seem too threatening with weapons?" asked Aithrod. "I only have throwing knives and a dagger, but Darium, you and Stone have swords. Stone even has a crossbow and staff. Mayhap we should leave the weapons behind."

"Nay!" cried Persimmon, having seen the battle. "We need to be able to protect ourselves if they should draw their weapons on us."

"She's right," agreed Darium. "I wouldn't enter the castle walls without protection."

"And I don't go anywhere without my weapons," Stone assured them. "However, I am not sure it'll matter. Once we are inside those castle walls, we could very well have an entire army opposing us, all with weapons drawn. If they decide to attack us, we won't be able to ward them all off. Still,

I'd feel better if you took my staff for protection, Aithrod."

"I will," said his friend, reaching out and patting the staff that he was already transporting on the side of his horse.

"I won't let it come to that," Darium assured them. "Besides, Sethor realizes that if they attack me, my brothers will both come with their armies in full array and he won't stand a chance against them. He also knows that there are magical beings in our family now willing to help us. He won't harm us."

"Let's hope you're right," said Persimmon, feeling her nerves shaking now.

They walked over the drawbridge, leading their horses and were stopped by two guards from the wall walk above.

"What do you want, Sin Eater?" called out one of the guards.

"I thought you gave up that nasty habit," said the other with a chuckle. "No one called for your services, Blackseed. Go home."

"I am not here to sin eat," explained Darium. "I come with my friends to seek an audience with King Sethor."

"He's not expecting you," said the one. "Go away. Send a missive instead."

"Let us pass," Stone commanded. "It is vitally important that we speak to your king. We have information he will want to hear."

"Tell us your information," said the one guard. "We will decide if he wants to hear it or not."

"Men, let them in," came a voice from behind the closed iron portcullis. "Raise the gate, anon."

Persimmon saw a man appear with an entourage of soldiers in his wake. He was an older but tall man with graying hair and a hooked nose. He wore a crown on his head, and was dressed in a fur-lined cloak and kingly attire. An assortment of jeweled rings decorated most of his fingers.

"Is that King Sethor?" she whispered.

"I am guessing so," Stone whispered back. "Whatever you do, don't leave my side. And be sure not to speak before you are spoken to."

"You are expecting trouble," she mumbled, thinking of the vision she'd glimpsed in his eyes.

"Just explaining court etiquette to you, sweetheart," he answered. "I don't want you doing anything to sour this man's disposition."

"I understand." She moved closer to Stone as they approached the gate. The men atop the wall walk worked the pulley and gears. With a loud creaking noise the heavy iron gate slowly lifted to allow them entrance.

"Leave all your animals outside my castle walls," commanded the king, raising his hand as they started forward.

"Why?" Darium demanded to know.

"I've seen what that fae wife of yours can do, Blackseed, or are you forgetting," sneered the king. "I won't have animals attacking me again. Especially not that damned bird of yours."

"My bird stays with me."

"Then you both can stay outside my walls. So leave."

"Nay, we can't leave," Persimmon told the king, rushing into the courtyard. She heard the rest of the men following after her. Panic filled her, thinking she wouldn't have the chance to find the old couples' son. She had seen how important this was to them. If they left now, she'd have to tell the dying couple that she'd failed. Persimmon didn't want to fail. And she certainly didn't want to let anyone down.

"What did you say?" growled the king.

"Dammit, I told you to stay by me, and not to speak," Stone ground out, coming up behind her.

"I can't leave before I find Gregor Lithum," she told the king. "His parents have been attacked by thieves and are close to death. Is Gregor here?"

"Who are you?" snapped the king, not even acknowledging her question.

"I am Persimmon Burroughs from Lornoon," she told him, followed by a curtsy. She looked at Stone from the corner of her eye, wanting him to know she was trying her hardest to follow court etiquette.

"Lornoon?" The king's hand moved to the hilt of his sword. "You come from the land of magic. You are a witch, aren't you?"

"Is that a bad thing?" she asked, her eyes flashing from the king to Stone and then over to Darium who had entered the courtyard but without his raven. If looks could kill, she'd be dead right now by all three of them.

"I don't like this," shouted the king. "This is a trick to take over my kingdom. Men, seize them and take them to the dungeon!"

"Go, Murk. Get help," shouted Darium, pulling his sword from the scabbard on his back. Stone drew his sword as well. Aithrod held out the staff with two hands. Fang snarled and showed his teeth as the raven squawked from atop a turret and took off into the sky. The men stood with their backs to each other, their weapons at the ready. Stone reached out and pushed Persimmon to the middle of their circle.

"Stay close, and don't think of disobeying me this time," Stone commanded.

"I can help," she said, but no one would listen to her. Swords started to clash as a battle began.

"It was a bad idea to come here," shouted Darium.

"I agree to that," said Aithrod, using the staff to ward off a blow from one of the king's soldiers.

"We were fine until the girl decided to open her mouth." Stone was not happy with her at all, and she hoped they'd live through this so he could forgive her later. A soldier ran toward them. Stone stepped in front of Persimmon, keeping her from being hurt.

"Everyone, start moving toward the gate," instructed Darium. "I hate to have to do this, but I'm going to use my fae power to blow them back and keep them away from us."

"I can help, too," Persimmon said again, but still no one listened to her.

They slowly moved toward the gate. Darium lifted his hand and started a whirlwind, keeping the men from moving closer.

"Get to the horses," shouted Stone. "We'll have to try another approach later."

Darium's fae power of controlling the wind was working to their advantage. They were almost out the gate and to the horses when Persimmon realized the pouch holding her crystal orb had fallen from her waist band during the struggle. She looked around and saw it laying on the cobblestones inside the court-yard. She couldn't leave it there. It was precious to her and the only remembrance of her mother.

"Get on your horses. Now," shouted Darium. "I'll try to hold them off."

"Let's go," Stone told her, turning toward the horse to mount.

"I can't leave it," she muttered, going after the crystal ball instead of following the men to safety.

Nine

"Up you go, Persimmon." Stone slid his sword back into his scabbard, and went to grab the girl and lift her up into the saddle. But when he turned around, she was no longer there.

"I can't hold them off any longer," Darium shouted. "I am still not used to my powers and get drained quickly. We need to leave here, now. Let's go."

"Wait!" Stone called to the other men. Darium had stopped controlling the wind and the soldiers were moving forward. He was already atop his horse. Aithrod was already riding away. "Persimmon isn't here," Stone said, but with all the noise and commotion, they didn't hear him. He looked through the settling dust into the courtyard from the whirlwind Darium created. That's when he saw Persimmon bending down to pick something up.

"We've got to go right now," yelled Darium. "What are you doing?"

"You two leave. Take Fang with you," shouted Stone. "I'm going back for the girl."

"Do you know what you're doing?" asked Darium.

"I sure hope so. Just get out of here. We'll meet up with you later." Stone rushed back into the courtyard, once again drawing his sword. "Persimmon, let's go!"

She stood up with that damned velvet bag in her hands that held her gazing orb.

"I couldn't lose this," she said, holding up the bag.

Stone reached out for her, but before he could pull her away, King Sethor grabbed her, holding his blade to the girl's throat.

"Drop the weapons or I'll slit her throat," warned King Sethor.

"What the hell else can go wrong?" muttered Stone, still holding on to his sword and looking back to the gate which the soldiers had lowered. It was too late. Darium sat atop his steed on the other side. There was nothing he could do to help them. Nodding to Darium, Stone threw down his sword and raised his hands in the air.

"Now, the crossbow, dagger, and hidden knives," ordered Sethor, holding Persimmon so tight that Stone heard the girl whimper.

"All right, just don't hurt her." He threw down the last of his weapons and held up his hands once again. "Now, release the girl."

"I'll release her, but the two of you are going straight to the dungeon." Sethor gave his men the command. The soldiers seized them both and hauled them away.

"We're not here to harm you," shouted Stone,

fighting against the hold of the soldiers. "I am here hunting down a thief and his counterpart. I believe they might be right here inside your castle walls. They're dangerous," he told the king.

Sethor laughed and nodded. Two men walked out to join him. "Do you mean my new soldiers?"

"Rancor Ruse," growled Stone, seeing the man he hunted along with another thief of Taelgonoth named Filip.

"Hello, Nightstalker." Rancor grinned, showing his rotten and broken teeth.

"You stole gemstones from King Helix. I swear I will bring you both in, and return the jewels to our king. Justice will be served."

"King Sethor is our king now," said Filip. "We serve only him."

"They'll steal from you as well, Your Majesty," Stone told Sethor. "Mark my words, they are bad to the core. You don't want anything to do with them."

"On the contrary, these men have made me an offer I cannot refuse," said Sethor.

"What's that?" asked Persimmon.

"We've promised the gemstones to King Sethor," Rancor told him.

"And what, pray tell, did you ask for in return?" asked Stone, knowing Rancor didn't do anything that didn't benefit him directly.

"Ruse is going to take me through the portal along with some of my soldiers so I can seize and rule Taelgonoth," Sethor told him with a chuckle.

"Nay!" shouted Stone, knowing this could be the worst thing that could ever happen to his homeland. "Don't believe Rancor," said Stone, fighting against the soldiers. "He is only out for himself. Besides, no one knows how to open the portal again or even if it'll ever be able to take us back to our homeland. You've made a bad deal."

"To the dungeon with those two," said Sethor with a flick of his hand.

"If you don't let us go, you'll have a war on your hands," Persimmon warned him. "Kings Rhys and Zann will be at your gates with their armies to save us. Not to mention, all the magical beings will be here as well."

"By the time they return, you two will be dead," said Sethor, laughing. "We're going through the portal to first seize the kingdom, then I'll gather up more soldiers in Taelgonoth so I can return here and take over the entire land of Mura as well. Don't you see? I'm going to be the most powerful man of two different lands."

"Or at least the greediest," mumbled Stone, not thinking anyone could be that blackhearted.

"Nay, wait!" shouted Persimmon. "You need us."

"Whatever for?" asked Sethor.

"Because, I have a crystal orb and I can see the future."

"So, you've got magic." This seemed to interest the king.

"Our king kills those with magic," one of the guards told her.

"Oh, no." Persimmon's worried gaze interlocked with Stone's. Her idea had backfired.

"Give me the orb." Sethor pushed forward and held out his hand.

"It won't do you any good," said Stone. "She is the only one who can use it."

"Then you'll use it to see my future, both here and through the portal, too," commanded Sethor. "And if you agree to do it, I'll let you live."

Stone was relieved to at least hear that they weren't going to kill Persimmon. But what he heard next was something he didn't want to hear at all.

"However, the bounty hunter is of no use to me. I'll kill him myself right now." Sethor unsheathed his sword and moved closer.

"Nay!" cried Persimmon, seeing that the king was about to kill Stone. She had to help him. She yanked the crystal orb from her pouch and pretended to scry. "It would be very bad for you to kill or even hurt the bounty hunter," she told him.

"What?" King Sethor lowered his sword slightly. "Why? Did you see something in that ball?"

"Kill him," snarled Rancor. "He's only going to make trouble for us all."

"Wait. Not yet. I need to know what the witch saw first." Sethor looked back and forth between them.

"The girl is lying," said Rancor's friend, Filip.

"Mayhap you're right. And I don't like to be fooled." Sethor raised his sword again.

"By killing Stone you'll be placing a death sentence on your own head from his king," Persimmon spat out, not really seeing a thing in the orb, but saying this to keep Stone from being murdered.

"How do I know you're not lying just to save his

hide?" asked the king. "Mayhap by letting him live, it'll bring about my demise instead."

"I only know what I see," said Persimmon. "The gazing ball never lies. However, it is up to you to determine what it means."

"Are you willing to risk it?" asked Stone. "After all, Persimmon does have some admirable powers."

"Yes. You are more powerful than I expected," said the king in surprise, slowly sheathing his sword. "That can be used to my advantage. Take them both to the dungeon, after all."

"What are you doing, King Sethor? You cannot really believe them." Rancor tried to discourage the king from letting them live.

"Persimmon. Do something," whispered Stone.

She knew she had to do something quickly to settle the king's mind and to make him believe what she said she saw was true.

"I see that Rancor is about to trip and fall," said Persimmon, rubbing the crystal ball, but not really seeing a thing within it. But to make them think what she said was the truth, she used her power of moving things with her mind. She took a deep breath and focused on Rancor.

"That is nonsense. She's a fake." Rancor took a step toward the king, and when he did Persimmon used her mind to push him down.

"Ooomph!" Her powers worked. Rancor doubled over and hit the ground.

"There is the proof you need, sire. The girl obviously can see the future," said Stone, giving her a quick nod of his head to thank her for what she did.

The king's eyes opened wide in surprise. "Put

them in the dungeon. And Rancor, if I hear another word about this from you or your friend, I'll take my sword to both of you instead." He turned to go while the guards escorted Stone and Persimmon to the dungeon.

"What now?" Stone whispered to her.

"Don't worry," she whispered back. "I have an idea." Persimmon took another deep breath and released it, only praying to herself that what she had in mind would really work.

Ten

S tone felt a knot in the pit of his stomach as the guards slammed the iron barred door of the cell, locking both him and Persimmon inside.

"Rot in there, the both of you." The guard chuckled as he hooked the ring of keys containing the one to the cell door to his belt and turned to walk away.

Stone was about to shout something back at the guard, but stayed silent when Persimmon placed her hand atop his arm. He looked over to her in question.

She smiled at him and nodded at the guard.

When Stone looked back at the guard, he saw the key ring lifting from the man's belt. It slowly floated right over to the cell door. Stone hurried over and stuck his hand through the bars and grabbed it. When he did, it made a jangling noise. The guard stopped and turned around.

"What was that?" asked the guard, looking around in a suspicious manner. "What was that noise I heard?"

Stone quickly hid the ring with the keys in one

hand, shaking the bars of the door with his other, making a loud rattling noise. "Let us out! Let us out, I say."

"Quiet down," shouted the guard, turning and leaving the dungeon.

"Your distraction worked." Persimmon hurried over to the door to join him. "Thank you."

"Nay, thank you for using your powers to get the key." With his hand through the gate, he used the key to unlock the cell, and slowly and quietly pushed the door open. "I still have no idea how we'll manage to walk out of here alive, but at least this is a start."

"Aye," agreed Persimmon, following him out of the cell. "If only one of us knew the layout and grounds of the castle, we might be figure out a path to use to escape."

"That's what I'm here for."

Stone looked up to see the pesky elf standing with his back against the stone wall and his arms crossed over his chest.

"Father!" exclaimed Persimmon. "You came to save us. Thank you."

"I'm only here at the request of Lira."

"Oh," said Persimmon, a frown washing over her face.

"How did you get here so fast?" asked Stone. "There is no way the others could have made it back to Kasculbough already, could they?

The elf gave him a strange look and shook his head. "You have no idea of my powers or of how fast I can really move, you big oaf."

"Oh, that's right," said Stone. "I've seen you disappear in a blur. But the others can't move that fast. There was no time for this all to transpire."

"The raven returned to tell Talia-Glen and Alaina that you two so stupidly managed to get caught. Rhys and Zann wanted to bring their armies to the king's door, but that would be an even dumber move right now. That's why I offered to come instead."

"Never mind all that. Can you get us out of here?" Stone scanned the dimly lit area, watching for the guards to return.

"I can. I used to work for King Sethor and I know every nook and cranny of this castle."

"You used to work here?" asked Persimmon, sounding just as surprised to hear this.

"Doing what?" asked Stone.

"It doesn't matter." The elf glowered at him. "Now stay quiet and keep close to me. We have to move fast. I know of a secret door that we can use."

"Thank you, Father." Persimmon liked the fact that instead of abandoning her again, now her father was there when she needed him. She hoped this was the start of a special change that could possibly create a bond between them.

"Don't thank me yet," said the little man. "Because, I swear if either of you do something stupid enough to get caught escaping, I will leave you both behind without a second thought."

"We won't," said Stone.

Persimmon knew the speed at which the elf could move. It would be easy for Elric to zip away and leave them both there to die and not have a second thought about it. She needed to be careful.

Sneaking through the dungeon, they stopped when they saw two guards sitting near the door at a table, playing cards.

"Damn, I'm going to have to distract them," mumbled the elf.

"Allow me." Persimmon looked toward the door and took a deep breath. "Get ready to run out of here."

Using her powers, the door to the dungeon slammed open and a breeze blew the cards off the table to the floor.

"Damn it," said one of the guards. "Get the cards, fast before Sethor finds out what we were doing."

When they bent down to collect them, Persimmon used her skill to make Stone's weapons that were on the table float over to them.

"Hey!" cried a guard, seeing what was happening.

"Take your weapons," she told Stone. "Quickly."

When the guards got up and drew their swords, she made their weapons fly out of their hands. Then she caused the wooden table to rise into the air and hit the men, knocking them down.

"Let's go," she told the others. The three of them quickly slipped out into the sunlight. Unfortunately, there were another couple of guards standing by a wagon filled with wine barrels, and they spotted them.

"Halt!" called one of the men.

"The prisoners are escaping," shouted the other.

"Let's go," said Elric.

"Wait." Persimmon squinted her eyes, looking toward the cart. Suddenly, it broke a wheel and the wine barrels rolled off the cart, hitting both of the guards. "Now, we go." She was about to turn around when she saw the ghosts of the old couple standing next to the broken wagon.

Gregor is in the keep, said the man.

Our son is here. You need to go to him. Please, contact him for us, said the old woman.

"We need to go into the keep. That is where we'll find Gregor," she told Stone and her father.

"No way. The only place you're going is out the secret door with us." Stone dragged her along with them, not allowing her to go back into the castle.

They made it to the secret door quickly, but Elric couldn't remember where to find the key.

"I know the hidden key is here somewhere." Elric patted the wall that was covered with ivy, but he couldn't find it.

"Can't you just whip up a key out of midair?" asked Stone impatiently.

"I could, but I won't," said Elric stubbornly. "That wasn't part of the plan."

"Oh, never mind. I've got it." Persimmon used her mind powers to open the secret door. Then the three of them slipped out quickly and she closed the door behind them.

"Hurry. Let's get back to Kasculbough before they start to follow us now that they are alerted that we've escaped," said Persimmon.

"I'll meet you there," said Elric.

"Nay, Father. We need you to find our way back. Please, don't abandon us. We are not familiar with this land."

"You'll find it," said Elric, sounding as if he didn't have a care in the world. "Just head for the waterfall and keep walking. Keep your eyes open for the castle. It's big. You can't miss it." Elric sped off in a blur, leaving Stone and Persimmon alone.

"I'm frightened," she admitted, not knowing what would happen.

"I'll protect you," Stone promised. "There is nothing to be scared about." He took her hand and they ran, trying to keep hidden in nature as they traveled.

Once Stone had voiced his promise to protect the girl, he realized how stupid it must sound to her. After all, even though Stone had his weapons again, he couldn't fight off an entire army. Persimmon was the one with all the power, not him. They stopped to catch their breath at the waterfall, looking over their shoulders, but thankfully not seeing King Sethor or his army of soldiers following them yet.

"It won't be long before they're upon us," said Persimmon, breathing heavy and sitting atop a large boulder to rest. "They will know we're headed back to Kasculbough and will know which path we've taken."

"We'll make it. We'll be fine, don't worry." Stone sat next to her. Together they looked at the gorgeous waterfall that fell from the top of the Pica-jord Mountains in a powerful stream down the rocks to the lake below. In the lake were floating lily pads and large ornate, brightly colored flowers that he had never seen before. Butterflies, dragonflies and those bees as large as birds all buzzed busily around the pond, dipping up and down into the flowers. Tall green evergreen trees and lots more lively, bright green shrubbery surrounded the entire area and led all the way up the tall mountain. He could just feel the life all around him, enhanced by the warmth of the bright sun. "This land of Mura is truly magical, and quite amazing," he said aloud in awe.

"Yes, I agree. Isn't it beautiful?" she asked, staring up at the falling water.

The roar of the falls filled the air, reminding Stone of how much power and energy nature held. Even in its finest hour, Taelgonoth had never felt like this. "It is," he replied. "We don't have anything like this back home."

"My mother often told me stories of Mura, and I know the names of all the places though I've never been here until now," she relayed the information to him.

"Why not?" asked Stone. "Is your homeland that far away?"

"Nay," she answered. "Actually, Lornoon is an island right across the channel leading from the Masked Sea. It can be reached from the west side of this island."

"I would like to see Lornoon someday. I'm sure it is as beautiful as this."

"Why do you say that?"

"Because," he answered, getting lost in the way her face lit up and she seemed to glow when she was around nature. "It has to be a special place since someone as lovely of you has lived there for so long."

"She looked over to him and smiled shyly. "You are too kind, Stone. Thank you for making me feel special. No one has ever made me feel this way before."

"Persimmon, I don't understand. Why did your mother shelter you in the abbey your whole life? And why doesn't your father seem to accept you? It makes no sense at all to me."

"I wish I knew the answer." She wiped a stray tear from her cheek. "I felt so alone and unloved my whole life, until I came to Mura. I just wish I had traveled here long before now." When she reached up to wipe away another tear, he used his hand to do it for her.

Persimmon looked up into Stone's eyes, feeling as if they belonged together. She longed for the intimacy of his touch. Just feeling him wipe away her tear gave her so much hope that because of him, her life could be so much better. His fingers gently glided across her cheek, sending a delicious shudder through her. Then he cradled her chin in his palm and his eyes settled on her lips. Before she knew what happened, he'd leaned closer and kissed her. Persimmon didn't stop him, because this was what she'd been waiting for. She liked it. The softness of his lips against hers was surprising. For such a hardened man who hunted other men for a living, he had a true gentle nature about him. Persimmon's eyes closed as the kiss lingered and then their lips slowly parted.

"Mmm, that was nice," she said, feeling safe and happy being with Stone. With him by her side she no longer feared anything.

"You are an amazing woman, Persimmon. Any

man would be lucky to call you his." He kissed her again, and she reached up and put her hands on his shoulders. And when he slowly pulled away, their eyes remained interlocked. She felt as if somehow they were joined together as one.

"I saw that coming," she admitted.

"What?" He chuckled. "How could you? You weren't even looking into your crystal ball."

"Nay, I wasn't. But yesterday I had a vision and we were kissing."

"Really. I guess there will be no surprises being around you." He stroked her cheek again, and she leaned into his touch.

Suddenly, they heard the noise of thundering hoofbeats rumbling the ground. The sound came from the direction of King Sethor's castle.

"Oh, no. They've found us." Persimmon jumped up, spinning around, looking for their captors to appear. "I'm not sure my magic is strong enough to be able to hold off an entire army."

"You won't have to. Come with me." He held out his hand and she willingly took it. But when he started walking toward the water, she became confused and stopped.

"What are you doing?" she asked. "We are going to the wrong way. We have to get back to Kascul-bough, not go for a swim at a time like this."

"We are returning to the castle, but first, we need to hide. We cannot outrun them on foot when they are atop horses. If they don't see us, Sethor and the others will ride right past us. It is our only chance to not get caught." He entered the water and pulled her along with him.

"Stone, I still don't understand what we're doing. I can't hold my breath under the water until they're all gone."

"And neither will you have to. Now, just trust me. Please."

"All right," she said, releasing a deep breath and nodding. "I do trust you." She flashed him a quick smile.

"Good. This way, then," he instructed, swimming toward the waterfall. Now, she understood.

"I'm coming," she told him. "I'm right behind you, Stone."

They made it to the other side of the small lake and had just climbed up the rocks and slipped behind the waterfall when King Sethor and his army of men rode up. They stopped for a moment, looking around.

"They must have gone this way," said Sethor. "Where in the world are they? Look everywhere."

"They're probably hiding," said Rancor.

"Then check behind every tree and bush. Hurry!" commanded Sethor.

Shaking from being wet and cold, Stone wrapped his arms around her. They were safe and protected behind the falling water, standing in a small cave in the rocks.

"Don't make a sound," he whispered directly into her ear, following his words with a small kiss.

She was afraid to even breathe, thinking somehow it would alert Sethor and his men to their presence. They were searching the area, but thankfully none of them had thought to look behind the waterfall.

"We are wasting too much time," called out Sethor. "They must be up ahead. Let's go."

In a puff of dust, the men atop their horses charged toward Kasculbough, leaving them and their hiding place undetected.

"It worked," she said as soon as she was sure they had all left. She was so cold that she couldn't stop her body from shaking or her teeth from chattering together. "They didn't see us. You are a life saver, Stone."

"Just a little trick I picked up in my profession."

"So, can we go now?"

"Not yet. And when we do, we're still going to have to be careful. We don't want them to spot us on their return trip to Macada Castle."

"How long do you think we should stay here?" she asked.

"However long, it wouldn't be long enough," he told her, once again leaning over to kiss her.

"The others will be worried about us," she told him. "We don't want them to send an army to Sethor's door looking for us."

"Nay. Of course, we don't want that." Stone looked out from the waterfall, and up to the sky. "It's clouding over and looks like it's going to storm. I think we'd better go."

"Aye, we wouldn't want to get wet, would we?"

He stopped and looked back at her and she started giggling. They both laughed at her jest, and it felt good. Persimmon liked having someone to share a jest with. Being with Stone Nightstalker felt like the first thing in her life that was right.

"Stone, how will we be able to avoid the soldiers?" she asked him. "Since Rancor is with him and he's a thief, he might figure out what we're doing."

"Leave that to me, sweetheart." He held her hand as they walked. "Remember, I am a tracker. We'll be able to tell which way they took and be sure to go far around their route."

"Thank you," she said. He stopped and looked back at her.

"For what?" he asked. "You were the one who saw to our escape. I should be the one thanking you instead."

"That's not what I mean," she told him. "Thank you for being kind to me. I haven't had a lot of kindness in my life and it feels nice."

"I promise you, Persimmon, that I will always treat you with love and respect. I will also do everything in my power to make sure that no one is ever mean to you again."

Eleven

The sky opened up and it started to pour just as Stone and Persimmon neared Kasculbough Castle. They could see the merlons of the strong castle walls connected by the turrets up ahead in the distance. It wouldn't be long now before they were crossing the moat.

"Stone, wait." Persimmon took him by the arm. "I think I saw that bush move up ahead. Someone might be hiding in it, waiting to ambush us." She didn't want to have gotten this far and then be captured again just outside the castle.

"I've been tracking Sethor and his men," Stone told her. "By the prints I found, and the broken twigs and branches, I believe they already returned to Macada Castle because of the approaching storm. We should be safe."

"Then why is that bush moving?" She pointed, and huddled up next to him.

He chuckled. "Fang, is that you?" His dog shot out from behind a bush. A rabbit darted past him when Fang emerged. The dog barked happily. "Come here, boy. I'm back, and happy to see you." Stone got down on his knees and the dog sped over, jumping up on him and licking his face.

"My, someone is happy to see you," commented Persimmon.

"Fang and I have been through a lot together. He is a loyal companion, just like Aithrod."

"There they are!" Darium rode over atop his horse, being followed by his brothers. His raven flew by above their heads, landing in a nearby tree. "We were just coming to look for you."

"Didn't my father tell you that we escaped King Sethor's prison?" asked Persimmon.

"He did. But he also told us that since you weren't back yet you were probably captured again," Zann answered. "I decided we needed to set out to find you."

"*Who* decided?" asked Rhys, giving his brother a dirty look.

"All right, so it was Lira and the women who urged us to come after you," admitted Zann. "But what does it matter? Here we are."

"Right," said Darium. "We didn't come sooner because I knew Stone would get you two out of there, so I wanted to wait and give you a chance."

"Good job, Stone." Rhys nodded. "You seem to be worth your salt."

"Thank you for your admiration, but I must admit that it wasn't me who got us here," Stone told him. "It was thanks to Persimmon's powers that we are alive right now." He smiled at her and winked, making her heart flutter.

"Impressive," muttered Zann.

"Well, let's get you both back to the castle by a warm fire and into something dry," suggested Rhys.

"What happened to King Sethor and his men?" Stone still scanned the area, never resting for a minute, always on alert.

"We'll fill you in later. Come," said Zann, just as a loud crash of thunder rattled the air, making Persimmon jump. "We're not far from the castle. Give me your hand, Persimmon. I'll give you a lift." He reached down for her.

Persimmon rode atop Zann's horse with him while Stone rode with Rhys. Fang followed close behind. They were greeted excitedly by the women as soon as they returned. After a good meal and having changed into dry clothes, the Blackseed brothers and their wives, as well as Stone, Persimmon, and Stone's friend, Aithrod, all gathered around the fire to discuss the happenings of the day.

"How are the old couple?" asked Persimmon. "I feel horrible that we weren't able to bring back their son with us."

"Mr. and Mrs. Lithum are still in critical condition." Talia handed Persimmon a goblet of wine. "Don't worry. I'm sure you'll find their son soon."

"Even if we do, I'm not certain he'll come to see his parents." Stone lifted a tankard. "I mean, if he's one of King Sethor's soldiers, he's most likely not going to be allowed to come here."

"Nay, I don't suppose so. Not after what happened today," agreed Darium, throwing a few crumbs to his raven. The bird hopped around atop the trestle table looking for more to eat. "We never should have gone inside the walls of Macada Castle.

It was a mistake. I should have known better. Things aren't the way they used to be since the death of two of Mura's kings. I need to remember that."

"Plus, you're not a Sin Eater anymore," said his wife. "Even if you were, King Sethor knows about all our magic, so it is understandable why you weren't welcome within his walls."

"King Drustan Grinwald of Evandorm and King Rand Osric of Kasculbough died and were replaced by Zann and Rhys," Medea explained to Persimmon.

"I see," she answered. "And it was a good thing, too. Were they just as evil as King Sethor?"

"You have no idea," answered Medea.

"I agree it was a big mistake to go to Macada Castle. Big." Elric appeared from nowhere as usual, climbing atop a bench. "Your stupid actions are now going to cause a war between Sethor and the rest of Mura. What were you fools thinking? The gods and goddesses of Mura are not happy about this at all."

"Who are the gods and goddesses?" asked Persimmon. "We don't have any on Lornoon."

"Yes, I'd like to know the answer to that, too," said Aithrod, eating as usual as he talked.

"We don't have deities on Taelgonoth, either," added Stone.

"I will answer that," said Talia. "Zoroct is the main god and the most powerful. He is god of power and might. Cnoir is the goddess of love and wealth, and Hapsren, who is my favorite, is the goddess of home and the hearth."

"Where are they? I haven't seen them," said Persimmon.

"They are not seen unless they want to be, which isn't often," explained Rhys.

"They can only be contacted by visiting the pyramids of the gods, which are temples to them," continued Talia.

"And where are these temples, or pyramids?" asked Stone.

"They're on the other side of the island. The magical side," said Elric. "Don't worry about it since you will never be going there. Now, back to the problem at hand. The war that you fools have obviously stirred up."

"Hah!" chuckled Rhys. "A war won't happen. Even if it does, we've got twice the amount of soldiers than they do. Not to mention, we have magic on our side now. If a war starts, we have no real chance of losing."

"Don't get cocky, Blackseed," warned Elric. "And don't think I'm going to risk my neck for the rest of you if a battle breaks out because I have no plans of doing so."

"It could happen, Rhys," Darium told his brother. "I mean, if King Sethor manages to take over the throne in Taelgonoth like he threatened to do, we will be at a disadvantage if he returns with help."

"Nay, we can't allow that to happen," said Aithrod, shaking his head. "If Sethor manages to get through the portal, kill our king, and return in command of King Helix's army, there will be many who will die. We need to stop this before it starts."

"It's already started," said Elric under his breath.

"You don't really think that this will really transpire, do you?" asked Talia.

"No one even knows when the portal will open again or if it'll appear in the same spot twice," Zann's wife, Lira pointed out.

"Don't say no one. Someone does know." Elric crossed his arms over his chest and glared at Persimmon. "Someone who can see the future, that is."

"Me?" Persimmon's heart leapt into her throat. This was the last thing she wanted to hear right now. These people needed help. Real help that she couldn't give them. She only wished that she could.

"Yes, you." Her father looked angry at her or mayhap it was disappointment. "You have Luna's gazing ball to see the future, so use it. What are you waiting for? You've said you've used it before."

"Yes, please do." Medea came to her side. "I'd like to find out just how your magic works. Mayhap you can even teach me to use it in time. I'd like that."

"If nothing else, you can tell us where to find Rancor when he's unprotected from King Sethor," added Aithrod. "That would help us out a lot."

"You can also tell us more about the son of the elderly couple. Mayhap if we can get him away from the king, he'll come to see his dying parents. Oh, do it, Persimmon, please," begged Talia. "We are all counting on you."

"I—I don't know." Persimmon looked down and ran her hand over the outside of the velvet bag feeling so nervous that she wasn't sure she wouldn't faint. She couldn't do what they were asking, but didn't want to tell them so. She had never actually told them she'd seen visions in the gazing ball precisely. Then again, she hadn't stopped them from thinking so either and now she regretted her action. They all depended on her for so much. In a way it was nice that someone needed her. Growing up, no one ever needed her and she felt so alienated. The only problem was they were counting on her for something she could not deliver. It terrified her and saddened her at the same time. She didn't know having friends and family would put her in such an awkward position.

"Please, sister." Lira's eyes showed desperation as she placed her hand on Persimmon's shoulder. "Don't push us away. Use your magic to help us. We're your family now. Family does not abandon each other."

Persimmon's gaze immediately flew to Elric. Her father was her family but had abandoned her just like her own mother had when she put her in the abbey. She was sure this wasn't the way family was supposed to act, but it was something she had no control to change.

Elric saw her looking at him and purposely turned his head the other way. She didn't care, she told herself. Just because her parents weren't there to teach her how family was supposed to support each other, didn't mean she should follow their ways and abandon the new family she had just found.

"Go on, it's all right." Stone looked over to her and smiled, making her feel as if he believed in her even though she knew she was about to let them all down. "Just hold up the crystal orb and look into it. You'll see the future just like you did when you saw us kissing."

"You kissed?" asked Aithrod in surprise.

"Oh, you kissed." Lira's face glowed. "How nice, sister."

Now Persimmon really felt uncomfortable. She didn't want everyone to know that she and Stone kissed. Her feelings for the man were private. And she really didn't want to have to pretend she saw something in the gazing orb when she didn't. My, how her deceit by first lying was getting her into a terrible tangled position.

"It is not that I don't want to help, it is because I can't control it," she blurted out.

"Can't control what? Yourself from kissing that big oaf?" asked Elric in disgust.

"Father, stop calling him that," Lira scowled at the elf. "Stone is our guest and we need to treat him with respect."

"That's right," agreed Zann. "At least until he's family. Then you can call him an oaf the way you do to me and my brothers."

"Enough with all this nonsensical jibber-jabber," snapped Elric. "Persimmon, use the orb to tell us what we need to know. Do it now. It is your destiny to step in and take over the skills of your late mother."

"Yes, Father," Persimmon found herself saying, only because she wanted to please the man and hopefully make him like her. She wasn't sure why this was so important to her, but it was. She'd always hoped to have a relationship with her father. One like he had with Lira. She wanted to feel close to him. And she longed to feel loved. It was something she'd wanted ever since she was a child. Now that her mother was gone, it was even more important to her than ever.

Persimmon plucked the orb from her pouch,

feeling her nerves shaking from the stress. Holding it up to her face, she took a deep breath and closed her eyes. What was she doing? She couldn't go through with this. Nay, she didn't want to deceive all these nice people. Persimmon couldn't fool them since they'd all been so kind to her. They were family. Her family. A family whom she respected and trusted. Didn't they deserve the same from her?

"Open your damned eyes and tell us what you see. You'll never see a thing that way!" scoffed the elf. "You need to gaze into the orb if you are going to scry. Or have you been lying to us and you really can't use it?"

Her eyes slowly opened.

"Don't let him upset you, Persimmon," mumbled Stone. "It's not worth it. Take your time. You can scry, can't you?" he asked the latter part softly, sounding as if he had doubt.

Her eyes slowly lowered to the cold gazing orb in her hand. It didn't surprise her to see nothing but a dark surface. She couldn't even see those confusing colorful swirls like she'd seen before. Nay, she had no power to scry and no right to pretend that she did.

As much as she wanted to look into the orb and tell her father that he needed to return the gemstones to Stone or something bad would happen, she couldn't do it. Her sense of being a moral person outweighed any feelings of acceptance she could possibly get from Elric. Stone was right. She shouldn't let his Elric's ill feelings for her upset her, even if she didn't know from where they came.

Her eyes slowly lifted to see her father's disapproving glare. Medea walked up behind her and stretched her neck to look into the crystal, seeming ever so hopeful to learn how to scry from Persimmon. The rest of them waited with curiosity and anticipation on their brows.

"Persimmon?" came Stone's deep voice. "Say something, please, sweetheart. Can you scry to help us or not?"

It was no use. The crystal was still dark and her mind was closed off completely. She couldn't even get a vision in her thoughts. She quickly returned the orb to her pouch and pulled closed the ties.

"I'm sorry," she said, hearing the quaver of her own voice. "I am sorry, but I'm not able to help any of you. And the last thing I wanted was to disappoint you." She took off at a run for the castle, not waiting to hear her father's comments, and not wanting to look at any of her new friends since she had failed to help them when they'd really needed her. They were all counting on her, and sadly, she had let them down.

"Persimmon, get back here," ground out her father.

"Sister, wait. What's wrong?" called out Lira.

Persimmon felt strong emotions bubbling up inside her. Struggling to hold back her tears, she needed to get away from everyone and just wanted to hide. She ran over the cobbled stones of the courtyard. Since she didn't want to be trapped inside the keep, so she looked for perhaps a garden instead to hide in. Hopefully there she would find solace and not have to face the others after the horrible episode that just transpired.

Not finding a garden of any kind, she ran toward what she first thought was a small pond. She stopped suddenly, almost losing her balance when she realized it wasn't a pond at all, but instead a huge hole in the ground. It was a pit of some sort that looked to her to be an enormous oubliette.

"Oh!" Her arms swam through the air as she struggled to keep her balance and not fall into it.

"Careful, Persimmon." Medea appeared in front of her, having used her power to transport to get there in the blink of an eye. She reached out and steadied Persimmon to keep her from falling into the pit.

"What is that?" she asked, pointing to the hole.

"It is a pit that was used to catch a dragon," Medea said without blinking an eye.

"A dragon?" That alarmed her. She quickly scanned the sky.

"The dragon is not here now, don't worry. It was from my homeland."

"So, you're not originally from Mura either?" Persimmon reached up and wiped away a tear from her cheek.

"Nay, I'm not. But that's not important. The only thing that matters is why aren't you able to scry?"

Her heart jumped. "What do you mean?" Persimmon sniffled and wiped away another stray tear. "Why would you say that?"

"Admit it. You want us all to believe you can see the future in the orb but you can't, can you?"

"How did you know?" It was almost a relief that Medea knew her secret. It made Persimmon not feel so alone anymore.

"I am not the only one who's been suspicious.

You keep ignoring my request to watch you scry and for you to teach me to do it. And you also ran away when we all needed your help just now, and didn't answer your father's question."

"Oh, Medea, you are right. I sadly don't have the ability to see the future like my mother did. I don't know why, but I just cannot do it. I am a failure. I am powerless, and I hate it."

"You are not a failure and far from powerless. You still have the ability to move things with your mind. We've already seen that."

"I do, but that's not enough. Now everyone will think I am a liar and a fraud. They will all hate me, just like my father does."

Medea rolled her eyes. "I'm sorry, but getting El-ric's approval should not be a worry of yours at all. And don't think that everyone will hate you, because they won't. Especially not him."

"Who?" Persimmon turned to find Stone run-ning after her.

"I will leave you two to talk."

"Nay, please stay with me, Medea." Right now, Persimmon didn't want to be alone with Stone.

"You need to tell him the truth, even if you don't reveal your lack of scrying to the others." Medea was gone in a flash, leaving Persimmon to face Stone on her own.

"Persimmon," called out Stone, running up to her. "What's wrong?" He stopped suddenly when he saw the big hole in the ground. "Don't stand so close to the edge of the oubliette. You might fall in." He put his arm around her waist and escorted her away from the pit. "What has you so upset? Was it something you saw in the gazing orb? Or was it your father?"

She paused for a moment before answering. Medea's words rang in her ears and she knew the girl was right. She had to let Stone know the truth. "Nay. I saw nothing in the orb. Nothing at all. That is what upset me." She took another deep breath and slowly released it, waiting for his response.

"Well, try it again. I'm sure it'll work now," he urged her. "It has to work. We need that information. Please, don't abandon all of us in our time of great need. The kingdom of Taelgonoth is counting on me to bring back the jewels and catch the thieves. I am in a foreign land and everything seems to be working against me. I can't complete my mission unless you help me, Persimmon."

It was going to be even harder now to tell him the entire truth. The rejection she was sure to endure when everyone discovered she couldn't scry to help them was going to be overwhelming. Persimmon had been through a lot lately and wasn't sure she could handle this. Oh, she longed for her mother right now. Her mother was the only one who could help her find comfort and tell her what to do. Even if she grew up without her mother for the most part, the times they did visit, her mother was always able to calm her down and even give her good advice on occasion.

"Take out the orb, Persimmon. Please, try again. Do it for me." Stone held on to her arm, looking into her eyes, believing in her even though he shouldn't. Then, he quickly kissed her on the lips, sending a surge of energy bolting through her. It was a good feeling, but at the same time only made things worse.

He cared for her. Stone was a good and kind man. He didn't deserve someone like her.

She fumbled for the orb, doing as he asked, but her hands shook so hard that the gazing sphere slipped through her fingers. It hit the cobblestones at her feet. Instead of shattering, it began to roll.

"I'll get it," offered Stone, but she shook her head.

"Nay. Only I can touch it." She didn't know what real difference it made, but it was something that she'd heard her mother say through the years. It was the reason her mother never let her try to scry. Or so she thought. Right now, she wasn't sure of anything. Persimmon hurried after the orb, bending down to scoop it up just as it stopped at the edge of the pit. When she hunkered down to get it, something caught her attention from the bottom of the oubliette. She slowly turned her head and looked down into the water that had settled at the bottom of the deep pit, probably from rain.

There, shimmering in all white was the ghost of her mother!

"Mother," she whispered, feeling her heartbeat pick up. She'd purposely left her homeland of Lornoon because she wanted to stop seeing the ghost of her mother. It was something that started happening right after the woman's death. It frightened Persimmon and also made her miss her mother deeply. To her surprise, it seemed that her mother's ghost had followed her here to Mura.

"What did you say?" Stone stopped right next to her, staring down into the pit. "Did you see something down there?" His hand was immediately on the hilt of his sword. "Don't worry, I'll protect you."

Even though Stone stared directly at the ghost of her mother, he couldn't see her.

"Stone, look hard. Tell me the truth. Do you see anyone down there?" Part of her was hoping that he could see the ghost, too.

"What? You see a person down there?" He stretched his neck to look. "Mayhap King Rhys has imprisoned an enemy. No one could escape such a deep pit. And since there is water in there, they could drown."

Persimmon, you are not alone. You have people who care about you, came her mother's voice from the pit. This surprised Persimmon. The ghost of her mother had never spoken to her before now. But she'd also heard the voices in her head of the old Lithum couple, so mayhap this was some sort of power she had and it was growing.

"Can't you hear her?" asked Persimmon, feeling anxious, frightened and worried.

"Her?" Stone made a face and continued to try to see the bottom of the pit. "I hope to hell Rhys didn't imprison a girl. I'll have to ask him about it."

You have to unleash the crystal orb's power in order to use it. Persimmon saw the ghost of her mother slowly disappearing. *You must help the others get the gemstones back where they truly belong. Their magic is powerful and cannot fall into the wrong hands.* The apparition disappeared and then the pit was dark again.

"Is something happening, Persimmon? Please, tell me what it is." Stone placed his hand on hers and stared deeply into her eyes.

"I did see something. Someone, Stone. But I am

not ready to speak about it yet." She stood up with the orb in her hand. "Please, don't say a thing about it to the others." She needed to think about what her mother just said. She had no idea how to the power of the gazing crystal or what her mother meant by saying the king's gemstones held magical powers.

"Hey, the orb seems to be glowing now," said Stone, his eyes fastened on the gazing ball in her hand. "Fast. Look within and tell me what you see."

"Huh?" She hadn't even noticed. Her attention dropped to the ball in her hand. To her surprise, once again she saw those swirling colors of blue, pink and orange. "Oh, I see those swirling colors again. They are so pretty."

"You must mean the portal, right? What else do you see?" Stone looked over her shoulder eagerly wanting to know more. You can scry, right?" he asked her again, sounding as if he wasn't sure if she could really do it.

Persimmon's excitement grew as the swirling colors started to part and the silhouette of a person actually started to appear but it was only a shadow. And then it all quickly disappeared as fast as it came.

"She doesn't see a thing. She's a liar, just like her mother." Elric's voice next to her only broke her focus and shook her nerves. Persimmon looked next to her to see her father with his rain of disappointment washing down upon her.

"Father, don't say that. Mother wasn't a liar." Her mother had been a good person and she wouldn't let anyone say otherwise.

"She was a liar, and so are you. I knew it all the time. Just admit it. You can't see a damned thing in that gazing orb, can you?" Elric crossed his arms over his chest and tapped his toe on the ground, waiting for her to answer.

"Don't speak to her that way," spat Stone, coming to her rescue. "Persimmon is a good and kind person and deserves respect. Quit calling her a liar. She has seen things in the gazing crystal and also sees something right now. Tell him, Persimmon. Tell him what you see."

By now, the rest of her new friends had hurried over to her, and crowded around her.

"What's going on, sister? Are you all right?" Lira was the first to get there.

"Shhhh, Persimmon is about to tell us what she sees in the gazing orb," said Stone, raising a hand in the air. "Please, sweetheart. Please, let this be true," he said to her in a mere whisper.

"Hrmmph! She sees nothing and has been deceiving all of us this entire time." Elric shook his head. "I'm not going to stay here and listen to any more lies. I'm leaving."

"Wait! I need my king's gemstones," said Stone, trying to stop him.

"The gemstones are not your king's and I will never let you have them." Elric dashed away in a blur.

"What did he mean by that?" asked Aithrod, hurrying over with the hound at his side. "The stones belong to our king. Why would he say otherwise?"

"What's happening?" asked Zann, walking up with his brother, Darium. Talia-Glen approached with Medea at her side.

"Quiet, everyone," Stone told them. "Persimmon

is about to reveal to us what she sees in the gazing orb."

"She is?" This came from Medea. "Persimmon? What are you doing?"

"Oh, tell us, quickly," begged Talia-Glen. "I can't wait to hear."

Persimmon looked back down to the orb but now she couldn't even see the pretty colors or that strange shadow of a person. There was nothing there at all.

"Please, tell us," said Stone. "Everyone is counting on you."

"Yes," said Aithrod from the center of the group. "We need to complete our mission and return to Tael-gonoth. Our king is depending on us to save his kingdom and we are depending on your visions to help us do it."

"We also need to find the elderly couple's son, don't forget," said Talia. "My herbs don't seem to be helping them. Alaina is with them now but said they probably won't live to see the morning."

With all the pressure building up inside her, Persimmon felt her head spinning. This was too much for her and she felt like she was about to snap.

"My father is right," she finally said, blurting it out before she could change her mind about doing it. "I am a liar," she admitted softly.

"Persimmon, no." Stone closed his eyes and shook his head slowly. "Please, don't say that."

"It's the truth," she told the group. "I have no power to scry, and never have. I wanted to impress all of you and especially my father. I wanted to feel special. To make you all like me. That is the only reason I pretended to be someone I am not."

"Oh, sister," cried Lira, sounding very sad. The rest of the group, including Stone remained silent. The dog whined and lay down with his nose between his paws.

It was happening already. Every one of them would start to despise her now and Persimmon realized that she had brought this all on herself. If she had just been honest with them all from the start, perhaps she would still have the adoration of her new friends and family. But sadly, after this, she realized she would once again be abandoned, rejected, and live the rest of her life alone.

"I don't feel well. Stone," she said, reaching out for him with one hand as her eyes closed and the dizziness overtook her. Any sound or sense of surroundings disappeared as Persimmon blacked out and entered a deep, dark, silent void that, to her, was worse than death.

Twelve

Stone laid Persimmon atop the bed inside the castle, glad he had been there to catch her or she might have fallen into the deep pit when she passed out. He wasn't sure what was going on with her, or why she said she couldn't scry when he thought she could. At first, he'd had his doubts about her. But she knew things, like what the old couple wanted and the name of their son and where to find him. She also told him she saw the kiss coming. That's why he started to believe that she could possibly really have the ability to see things in that gazing ball, after all. His heart went out to her because he knew she was going through something and he felt helpless to guide her through it. He had wanted so badly to believe she wasn't leading everyone on since he'd seen her use powers to move things with her mind. But now, he became confused and didn't know what to think about the girl.

"Stone?" Persimmon shifted atop the bed, her eyes opening slightly as she looked for him. "Don't leave me."

"You're safe, darling. Don't worry," he told her, taking a seat on the side of the bed. Even if she had been deceitful and fooled them all, he couldn't leave her. He had promised to protect her, and he would not go back on his word.

Alaina rushed into the room along with Lira, Medea and Talia. Aithrod slowly followed. Fang brought up the rear.

"Let me see her." Alaina brought forth a basket of herbs and potions. Stone got up and moved out of the way.

"Sister, what's wrong? Why did you faint? Are you ill?" Lira went around the other side of the bed and took Persimmon's hand in hers.

"I saw my mother," mumbled Persimmon, still seeming half-unconscious.

"I thought her mother was dead," said Stone, wondering if she had been dreaming.

"Shhh, let's hear what she has to say. Go ahead," Lira urged her. "What happened, sister? It's all right. You can tell us."

"I see ghosts," said Persimmon, sounding like she really meant it.

"Ghosts?" This surprised Stone. He wasn't even sure he believed in ghosts. "Mayhap she's just ill and hallucinating," he told the others.

"Nay," said Persimmon, still holding her sister's hand but looking straight at Stone. "I also have no ability whatsoever to see anything in a gazing orb and I am sorry to let you all think I did."

"No, Persimmon. That can't be true," said Stone, holding on to the last thread of hope. "You've seen us kissing. You told me so."

"I saw it, but in a vision in my mind, Stone. I never scried to know that."

"Oh, Persimmon," he said, his heart dropping. Too upset to think, he paced the floor.

"I am a liar and a fake. Just like my father said." Her eyes closed and Stone saw pain contort her face. "Now, you all know the truth. I deserve to have you hate me, just like Elric does."

"So she has no power to scry at all?" asked Lira.

"It's true," said Medea. "She has no skill to use the gazing orb and has just been pretending. She told me in confidence, but now that she has admitted it aloud, it is no longer a secret."

"Why would she do such a thing?" asked Aithrod. "I was hoping she could use her powers to help us get back home."

"I really hoped she'd be able to help us heal the Lithums," said Talia.

"I'm sorry I let you all down." Persimmon's eyes opened again and she looked straight at Stone. "I have never really had friends before I met all of you. I only wanted you all to like me."

Stone's heart went out to the girl and he stopped pacing. He had seen the way Elric treated his own daughter and he felt sorry for her. Her mother was dead and she was in a strange land now, just like he was. However, she'd made them all look like fools and he didn't like that. "We do like you, Persimmon. You don't have to try to impress us with lies about scrying and using the crystal when I know you have powers to move things. I've seen it myself."

"I'm sorry," she told him.

"I'm sorry, too. Now, I have a job to do and must

leave to get it done. I have to track down a couple of thieves." Stone turned to go, but her words stopped him.

"Gregor Lithum is approaching the castle right now."

"What?" He turned and scowled at her. "What are you saying?"

"The old couple just told me."

"Those elderly people are not even conscious and you've been nowhere near them today. Stop pretending like they are giving you messages. The game is over, sweetheart. Don't keep making up lies, because we don't like it." Stone was tired of playing this game and wanted it to stop.

"I'm not lying!" She struggled to sit up, and the women helped her. "I see their ghosts right now. They are standing right behind you."

"Enough!" He turned to go, and took a step, but stopped suddenly. It was as if a cold breeze had just blown right through him.

She's telling the truth he heard a man say.

Stone whirled around to face the others. "Who said that?"

"What do you mean?" asked Talia. "No one said a thing."

"I distinctively heard a man say she is telling the truth."

"It was Gregor's father," said Persimmon. "He also just walked right through you."

Stone's hand went to his chest. So that breeze he felt was a ghost going through him? And ghosts really did exist after all? This was all too much to take in. He turned and left, hurrying out of the room with Aithrod and Fang right behind him. They needed to continue their hunt for Rancor. This was all naught but a huge distraction, slowing him down. When he got to the courtyard, he saw the Blackseed brothers talking to some man who looked like one of Sethor's guards by the way he was dressed. The man sat atop a horse and the Blackseeds all held their swords out, aimed right at him. The man had his hands in the air and his weapons were on the ground.

"What's going on?" asked Stone, running over to the others.

"My parents are dying and I must see them," said the man. "My name is Gregor Lithum."

"Gregor Lithum?" Stone's body stiffened. So Persimmon was telling the truth about seeing the ghosts after all. Perhaps she wasn't as big of a liar as he thought.

"You're one of Sethor's men," said Zann.

"Yes, but I come unarmed," he said with a nod. "I don't want to fight. I just need to pay my last respects to my parents."

"How do we know this isn't a trap?" asked Rhys, being cautious.

"How do we know you are really Gregor Lithum?" asked Darium, bringing up a good point. He could just be pretending as part of an ambush. Mayhap Sethor and his men were right behind him. Possibly everyone was lying. Stone no longer knew.

"I saw some of you at Macada Castle earlier," said the man with his hands still raised. "I saw the Sin Eater, and you," said the man, nodding at Stone. "You have a witch with you who had a gazing crystal.

There was one more man with you as well as a dog and a raven."

"That's right," said Stone.

"It still doesn't prove you are who you claim to be." Zann told him. "I'm sure there were a lot of people there who know what you just told us."

"Do you think this is a trap being laid by Sethor?" Rhys asked his brothers.

"Nay," said Stone, speaking up. "Persimmon just told me inside that the ghosts of the elderly couple spoke to her and said Gregor was at the gate. It must really be him."

"The ghosts?" all three of the Blackseed brothers said together.

"My parents are ghosts?" asked the man atop the horse. "Please, tell me I'm not too late. Have they already died then? I need to speak to them. I haven't seen them in years. I want to ask their forgiveness."

"Now's a fine time for urgency," said Rhys. "If you really are their son, why didn't you come to see them sooner?"

"Why are you even working for Sethor?" added Darium.

"My parents begged me not to be Sethor's soldier," said the man, sadness washing over his face. "I only did it to be able to feed them and care for them. I sent them money to buy food every week. I had hoped to join them again someday, but King Sethor wouldn't allow it. He threatened to kill my parents if I ever went to meet them or if I ever left his service."

"Yet, here you are now," said Zann, still sounding suspicious.

"I heard these men say my parents are close to death, so what does it matter?"

"He is who he says he is." Stone was sure of it. "Persimmon said he'd come. I never should have doubted her word."

"Can you take me to my parents? Please?" asked the man. "I don't want them to die before I can tell them I am sorry."

"Are you sure about this?" Rhys asked Stone.

"I am," he answered. "I will take full responsibility for the man."

"All right, lower your arms, men. Gregor, get off the horse," said Rhys. "Follow Stone inside to see your parents one last time, but your weapons stay here."

"Thank you so much." Gregor slid off his horse and hurried over to Stone. "I am also sorry for everything King Sethor has done to any of you. I swear, I never wanted to stay there this long to serve him, but was frightened of what he'd do to my parents if I left."

"We need to hurry if you want to say your final goodbye," Stone told him.

"Let's go." Gregor hurried behind Stone as he led the way to the chamber where the old couple were being kept. Stone opened the door and stopped in his tracks, seeing Persimmon and the other women standing at their bedside. Talia was crying.

"This is Gregor, the old couple's son," announced Stone.

"Mother! Father!" Gregor ran to the bedside.

"I'm sorry," said Alaina. "We tried to help them but their injuries were too severe."

"That's right," said Medea. "We are glad you came, but I'm afraid you are too late, Gregor. Your parents have just passed away."

"Nay! Please." The grown man threw himself over the bodies of his departed parents and cried. "I am so sorry I didn't come sooner. I feared King Sethor would harm you if I did. I should have listened to the two of you. I am so sorry I ever worked for such an evil man. Please forgive me. Please." He cried and rocked back and forth, staring at the old couple.

"They say goodbye and that they love and forgive you." Persimmon looked over his head. "They are standing right behind you, Gregor."

"What?" The man looked up at her in confusion.

"I can see them and hear them," she continued.

"Stop it!" shouted Gregor. "You are lying. My parents are dead."

Persimmon looked crushed that the man should say this to her.

"Nay, she's not." Stone stepped forward. Persimmon's eyes locked with his. He could tell she'd been crying. "I can vouch for her and assure you that she is telling the truth." Stone made his way over to the bedside. "Persimmon can see and speak to ghosts."

"Then you believe me, Stone?" Persimmon blinked away a tear. "You really believe me?"

"I do," he said, laying his hand on his shoulder. "And I am sorry to have ever doubted you."

"Nay," she said, shaking her head. "I gave you cause to doubt me when I was first mistaken and thought to have scried and never corrected the misunderstanding."

"That's all in the past now, sweetheart. We don't need to dwell on it anymore."

"Then it's true. My departed parents really said they forgive me?" Gregor looked up and Persimmon nodded.

"They say they understand what you did and why you did it. They are thankful that you gave up everything to help them. But they also are telling me that they don't want you to work for King Sethor anymore. They worry about you, Gregor."

"I won't," promised the man, taking one of each of his dead parents' hands in his. "I promise you, Mother and Father, that I won't ever help that evil man again."

Darium, Zann, and Rhys entered the room. Darium carried a cloth bag with him.

"They also want Darium to sin eat for them so they won't go to The Dark Abyss," said Persimmon.

"Yes, please, Sin Eater. Please help them so they can get to The Haven where they belong for the rest of eternity," begged Gregor.

"I am here to do so." Darium pulled bread and a bottle of wine from the bag.

"Nay, Darium, don't risk it," begged his wife.

"Talia, I want to do this," said Darium. "Not for the dead couple, but for the peace of their son."

"Thank you." Gregor let go of their hands and stood next to the bed. Darium place bread atop the dead woman's chest, as well as the bottle of wine.

"May all her sins be forgiven, and may she find her way to The Haven where she will spend the afterlife in peace and comfort," said Darium, eating the bread and taking a swig of wine. Then he repeated the same process with the dead man, saying the words again. Stone had never seen anything like this in his life. It was either ingenious, or they were all a little crazy.

"They will make it to The Haven now," said Darium, when he had finished. "You don't have to worry for your parents anymore."

"There is a graveyard right outside the castle walls," explained Rhys. "My brothers and I will help you bury your parents."

"Thank you," said Gregor. "I am only sorry I stayed away so long. Are they still here?" he asked Persimmon.

Persimmon looked around the room and slowly shook her head. "Nay, I'm sorry. They've moved on," she told him. "But they were glad you came."

"I am so thankful," said Gregor. "I will do anything at all to show all of you how much I appreciate everything each of you has done for my parents. They meant the world to me."

"Anything?" asked Stone.

"Yes."

"Then help us sneak back into Macada Castle to capture two thieves from my homeland and to recover my king's jewels that were stolen."

"Stone, nay. You can't ask him to do that," said Medea. "It's not right. If King Sethor finds out he even came here now, he'll most likely order the man killed."

"I'll do it," said Gregor without a second thought. "I will gladly risk my life to help all of you. But, please, tell me something that I need to know. Who was it that killed my parents?"

"The same two men we are hunting down," answered Aithrod, walking into the room with Fang at his side. "The thieves of Taelgonoth."

"I will kill them with my bare hands if need be, but they will pay for taking the lives of innocent people." Gregor's fists clenched and he gritted his teeth. "They will not get away with this."

"Nay, they won't, I promise you that," Stone told him. "I will see to it personally. They will pay for their evil acts, and I will make sure justice is served."

* * *

Later that day, Persimmon rode atop a horse along with Stone as they made their way through the village of Kasculbough, and along the beach of the Masked Sea with Fang leading the way. The sun shone down upon them, warming her body and making her feel safe and secure. Puffy white clouds floated lazily in the bright blue sky above them. Crystalline waves drifted up to the shore, rippling the bronze field of smooth sand before them.

"It surely is beautiful in Mura. We very seldom have a bright sunny day in Taelgonoth," Stone told her.

"Really? Why not?"

He shrugged. "It is a much darker place than here. Sometimes, it is so bleak that it is hard to remember if it is day or night. And because of the lack of sun, not much grows. What we do have is mostly tangles of weeds or gnarled trees."

"Oh, my, that sounds awful. No wonder there is no magic there. I don't think a fae or elf or even a witch would live in a land without sun and flora. It is what we thrive on."

"It might not be as colorful or as beautiful as this land, but still it is my home and I miss it."

"Do you have family you left behind?" she asked him, wanting to know more about this intriguing man.

"No. Not anymore," he told her sadly. "Most of my family was killed off by a plague that swept through the land. The rest of them were killed in war. The same thing happened to Aithrod with his family."

"Oh, I'm so sorry," she told him, feeling his own sadness and emptiness in her heart. "So you have kingdoms fighting over there as well as they do here?"

"I am sure every land has greedy men who want to rule and will do anything to gain power. It is no different than anywhere else."

"Thank you for asking me to go for a ride, Stone, but it wasn't necessary," she told him, enjoying the closeness of their bodies pressed together as they traveled slowly along the beach.

"It's the least I could do to try to make it up to you that I didn't believe you when you said you saw ghosts. I'm sorry. I'm not used to all this magic and odd happenings."

"It's all right. Seeing spirits isn't a common thing."

"I heard that Darium had some experiences with the dead as well, but he wouldn't elaborate on it."

"Stone, can we stop and walk? I'd like to talk," she said, not wanting to have to keep looking over her shoulder to speak to him.

"Of course, we can." He stopped and dismounted and then aided her, slowly lowering her to the ground. The touch of his hands around her waist felt intoxicating. She couldn't stop from thinking about the kisses they'd shared. She wanted more than anything to experience that again.

As if he could read her mind, he leaned over and kissed her passionately on the mouth. Her arms closed around him and she returned the kiss. With their lips pressed together, Persimmon felt as if she hadn't a care in the world. All that mattered was that she found the man she wanted to love. Meeting Stone seemed to fill an empty void in her heart. She liked being around him. He was special.

Fang ran up to them barking playfully.

"What does he want?" she asked.

"He wants my undivided attention. Here you go, boy." Stone picked up a stick and flung it into the water. Fang darted off after it, splashing in the waves to retrieve it.

"I can understand the dog wanting your attention," she said, smiling at him. "I'm sure there are many girls back in Taelgonoth who would like your undivided attention as well."

"I wish I could say that is true, but it isn't."

"No?" she asked in surprise. "Why not?"

Fang returned with the stick. Stone stopped talking and threw it once again. The dog ran off after it, diving into the waves and swimming happily in the sea.

"I suppose it's my own fault for not wanting to get close with a woman," he told her. "But after losing everyone I ever loved, it just feels kind of—"

"Devastating," she answered for him. "And sad and lonely."

"Yes, I suppose so," he said, running his hand along the side of her face. She leaned into him, basking in the glory of his gentle touch.

"What I was going to say was that it feels freeing not to care about anyone like that anymore." He stared out over the water, seeming to be in deep thought.

"You really mean that?" she asked, surprised to hear him sounding so heartless.

"I do," he answered.

"You had a woman who you loved and lost. A girlfriend or perhaps a wife," she said, blurting it out before even thinking about what she was doing.

"What?" His eyes sought out hers. "Nay. Why would you say that?"

"Because you look like you are in deep thought."

"I am," he admitted. "But not for the reason you think."

"Then what is it? Please, tell me."

He hesitated for a minute and then let out a deep breath. "King Helix said when I return with the thieves and his gemstones, he will reward me by giving me his daughter Annabelle's hand in marriage."

"Oh," she gasped in surprise. She hadn't seen this coming. Persimmon dropped her hands from him and slowly pulled away. "I'm sorry."

"What are you sorry for?" He gave her a crooked smile.

"I was kissing you when you are betrothed to someone else."

"I am not betrothed yet," he told her. "Besides, I never agreed to marrying the girl."

"Why wouldn't you?" she asked. "You'd be married to the daughter of a king. It sounds like good security and a safe and secure life to me."

"Aye, it certainly would be," he agreed, getting that faraway look in his eyes again. "It is a wonderful offer that only a fool would reject." He continued to walk down the beach and she hurried to be next to him.

She seemed to have ruined the mood and was kicking herself for doing so. She never should have asked him so many questions about his life. The dog dropped the stick at their feet, Fang's tongue hanging out. She swore the hound was smiling. His white fur was wet and matted down but he looked so refreshed from the water. Stone bent down to pick it up but she was faster.

"Let me." She scooped up the stick and when she did, Fang jumped on her and knocked her down. "Oh!" she cried, her body hitting the water with a loud splash.

"Fang, bad boy!" Stone scolded the hound.

Sitting in the waves, Persimmon started laughing. "It's all right. The water feels refreshing and I am sure Fang just wanted me to feel it, too. Don't scold him. He was just playing." She threw the stick into the deeper water and Fang jumped in, swimming after it.

"Let me help you up." He reached out for her, but his mood was still soured. Taking a chance, she giggled, pulling him into the water with her.

"Aaaah!" He came splashing into the sea right

next to her. "That wasn't funny," he said, spouting out a stream of water and hitting her right in the eye.

"You are wicked," she said with a giggle, rubbing her eye. With her free hand she scooped up water and threw it at him.

"You have no idea how wicked I can really be." He grabbed her wrists when she tried to splash him again. They both laughed, and the mood changed from solemn to happy quite quickly. Then he knocked her down on her back, and straddled her in a sexual way, his long, wet hair hanging down around him as he leaned over and kissed her passionately right there on the beach. The waves washed over them, making Persimmon feel so delightfully naughty. It wasn't a feeling she was accustomed to, having grown up in the convent, but it was one she could get used to very quickly. His hand roamed down her chest and slowly slid over to her breast. He cupped her and gave her a light squeeze. Heat grew in her belly. He continued to kiss her and fondle her and it brought Persimmon to life. Still straddling her, he used his arms to hold himself up, pressing his hardened manhood against her belly, making her squirm beneath him in anticipation. Excitement filled her, and she found herself wanting to make love with this man.

"Mmm," she cooed, enjoying the intimacy between them. "I love your kisses."

"So, have you had many to compare them to?" he asked, kissing her once again.

She answered with her eyes closed. "Nay. Just yours."

"Really?" There was silence that followed and she

slowly opened her eyes to see him staring at her with hooded eyes.

"What is it, Stone?" she asked him. "Why did you stop?"

"You've never been with a man before?"

"Nay," she admitted.

"And how old are you?"

"I'm twenty-five. How old are you?"

"Twenty-eight."

"And you're not married," she pointed out.

"Neither am I still a virgin," he mumbled. "Damn," he swore under his breath, pushing his wet hair out of his eyes. He got up and pulled her along with him.

"Is it so shocking that I'm still a virgin?"

"It is, where I come from. Most girls are married by the time they are sixteen and have three or more children by their early twenties."

"It is like that where I come from, too," she said, wringing the water out of her long, black hair. "However, it was different for me because I grew up in a convent. I am an only child and my mother had me out of wedlock. She told me she had no choice but to put me in a convent so my reputation wouldn't be sullied like hers."

"But you're a witch. Did the nuns know that?"

"They didn't know or they never would have taken me."

"So they never saw you use magic?"

"Nay." She shook her head. "Never. If they had, they probably would have burned me at the stake."

"If this is true, how can you blame Elric for never

visiting you?" He took her hand and also the reins of the horse and they walked.

"Something went on between my parents that really affected them both. However, I could never get a straight answer from either of them what it was. I still don't know why my father never married Mother."

"Can't you ask Elric?"

"Do you see the way he is around me? Especially when my mother is mentioned?" She raised her brows. "I think he'd rather walk through fire than tell me anything that involves him and my mother."

"Well, mayhap someday that will all change."

Persimmon felt a buzzing vibration and an odd warmth coming from the wet pouch at her side. "Stone, wait a minute. Something is odd here." She dug out the orb and held it up. Her jaw dropped. "I can see those swirling colors again in the gazing ball. I really can, I'm not lying."

"Why sound so shocked?" he asked. "After all, you've seen crazier things. Like ghosts."

"Nay, this is the most amazing," she said, straining her eyes, trying to see the silhouette like before but she couldn't. "Stone, I almost feel as if I am on the verge of scrying. I don't how or why, but it almost seems like it might actually happen."

"I don't understand. Can't all sorceresses scry? I mean, isn't it something you would have inherited from your mother?"

"I am not sure. But it seems like in the last few days I've been seeing the start of something. I guess, since I am half elf, there is the possibility I can't inherit her magical abilities, at all."

"But you are seeing something in the orb now," he pointed out. "Why is that, if you don't have the ability to scry? I don't understand."

"I just remembered something that the ghost of my mother told me."

"What is that?"

"That the orb only works if its power is first unleased."

"And how do you do that?" he asked.

"I'm not sure, but I have an idea." She put her finger to her mouth in thought. "The last few times I've seen the swirling colors in the orb is when I was with you. Especially after you kissed me."

"Really?" He seemed interested. "So our kisses somehow spark the orb to life?"

"It could be."

"Shall we try it again? To see if it works, I mean."

She smiled and wet her lips with her tongue. "I won't stop you. As an experiment, of course."

"Of course." He cradled her cheek in his large palm and kissed her ever so gently. "Is it working?" he asked, his face still up against hers.

"I don't know. I can't see it."

"We'd better try a few more kisses, just to make sure its power was unleashed."

She didn't stop him from doing just that. His kisses were sensuous and downright alluring. And when his tongue parted her lips and entered her mouth, she felt a stirring below her belt that she'd never had before. A part of her seemed to be coming to life and she liked the way it felt.

"Let me look now," she said, her lips up against his as she spoke, her eyes still closed. The warm breeze kissed her skin and the sweet smell of wildflowers filled the air.

"Not yet," he whispered, his hands slipping around her waist, and then trailing lower until he cupped her buttocks in his palms. And when he pulled her tightly up against his groin, a buzzing sensation from the orb scared her and she dropped the crystal.

"Oh, my," she said, pushing away from him.

"I'm sorry. Did I go too far? I didn't mean to offend you."

"Nay, I loved it, Stone." She looked to the ground. "I was startled when the gazing orb started to vibrate in my hand." She hunkered down to pick it up. When she brushed the sand off of it, she actually saw a vision emerging in the orb. "Stone, look! Can you see it? I see something in the orb."

"Where?" he asked, leaning over the orb, holding her hand in his. "Nay, I don't see a thing."

"Mayhap, I'm the only one who can see it, since I'm a witch."

"What is it? What do you see?"

"It looks like...oh, no! It's Fang. He's in terrible trouble!" Her head snapped up and she looked out in the water for the dog. "There, I see him." She pointed far out in the waves. "The current must be too strong and he can't get back to shore. It's my fault. I threw the stick and now he's going to drown."

"Stay here," Stone told her, removing his tunic, exposing his broad, bare chest. "I'll get him." He kicked off his shoes and ran, diving into the waves, making his way toward the dog.

Persimmon watched nervously, hoping that Stone

was a strong swimmer. She prayed that he could save the poor dog. If his hound drowned, she would never forgive herself for being so careless.

"Show me what happens," she said to the orb, shaking it and trying to get another vision in it. It remained dark. Her asking it to give her a vision did not work at all. Anything she'd seen before was now gone. She quickly slipped the orb back into her pouch and kicked off her wet shoes, holding up her gown and running down the beach, making her way to Stone and Fang.

"Do you have him? Stone, are you all right?" she yelled into the wind. She wanted to jump in and swim after them, but she wasn't a good swimmer. Being in the convent for most of her life, she was never allowed to experience things that most girls her age could do. She'd only been able to practice swimming the few times she snuck out of the abbey to bathe in the lake. "Stone, do you have him?" she called again, barely able to see his head out on the water. Tears filled her eyes. This couldn't be happening. Everything had been going so well, and now it was about to end in tragedy. She prayed that it would not.

Falling to her knees, she squeezed her eyes closed and prayed once again the way the nuns had taught her. She asked that Stone and Fang would return unharmed.

"Persimmon, what are you doing?" she heard after a short while. Her eyes popped open. Stone emerged from the water, half-naked and wet, carrying the drenched dog. He looked like a water god emerging from the sea.

"You saved him! You're both all right." She

jumped up and ran to Stone, throwing her arms around him and the dog as soon as they got to shallow water. "Thank goodness you are both alive." She kissed the dog. Fang licked her face before squirming out of Stone's hold. He shook, getting them all wet, but Persimmon didn't mind.

"Fang gets a kiss but not me?" Stone asked playfully. "I'm the one who risked my life to save the mutt."

"I'll gladly give you a kiss, too," she answered, throwing her arms around him and kissing him over and over again.

He laughed. "Keep that up, and the gazing orb is going to explode."

"Let it," she said with a devilish grin, wondering in her mind what she'd be able to see in the globe if they actually had made love.

Thirteen

S tone knocked on the door to Persimmon's room the next morning, hearing her voice call out from within.

"Come in."

"Persimmon? Are you up?" He cracked the door and peeked inside, but didn't see her. "Sweetheart?" He entered the room fully, getting the air knocked out of him as Persimmon barreled into him, throwing her arms around him, kissing him hard on the mouth.

"Oomph!" He chuckled, taking her in his arms. "What was that for?"

"Come in and close the door. Quickly," she told him.

"What? Why? I was just going to leave to track down the thieves." He pointed out into the corridor.

"This is more important. And if it works, you won't need to look for the thieves because I will be able to tell you anything you want to know."

"What does that mean?" She was acting odd this morning and he wasn't sure what she had in mind.

"Close the door. Please."

"All right." With one arm still around her, he reached out for the door with his other hand and slammed it closed.

"I was thinking about it all night and I finally figured out the answer."

"You did? What answer? What was the question?" he asked, still very confused.

"Quickly, undress." Her hands went to his weapon belt to help him.

"Wait. What? Why?"

"Each time we were together, and especially when you kissed me, I was closer and closer to actually being able to scry."

"So?"

She stopped unbuckling his belt and looked up at him. "So, that means coupling is what will activate the orb and also my ability to scry." She pulled off the belt and weapons and laid them on a table.

"Persimmon, this is crazy. You are telling me that if we make love, somehow you will acquire the power to scry?"

"That is exactly what I mean. It has to be what unleashes my power. It all makes sense now. And I also think my mother was frightened for me and that is why she put me in the convent. She knew that being there I'd never acquire my scrying power." She started pulling his tunic over his head but he stopped her.

"I know men don't normally think this, but don't women usually want to be in love before coupling with a man?"

"We don't have time for us to fall in love, Stone." She gave up on him and started to remove her own clothing. "I can help you find the thieves and collect the king's gemstones, I know I can. All I have to do is unlock the orb's power and then gaze into it. I'll be able to see the future and know what any of us should do in any dire situation. Don't you see? This will help everyone. I'm sure this must be how it works. So we need to make love. Now."

"It'll help everyone," he repeated, trying to take it all in.

"Don't even try to talk me out of it because I've decided this is what I want to do to help you." She dropped her gown to the floor, standing there only in her shift.

"Do you even know for sure that this will really unlock your power? I mean, what if we make love and it does nothing at all to help you scry?"

"That won't happen," she said. "And even if it does, I won't regret trying. Will you?"

She removed the last of her clothing, standing there in front of him looking like a naked goddess. Suddenly, his mind was fuzzy and he couldn't think straight. Lust overtook him and his aroused form strained against his breeches. What he wanted more than anything right now was to make love with this beautiful, fantastic, lovely, but crazy woman.

"Well? Will you do it? Please?" she asked, batting her long lashes, looking even more seductive with a little pout on her lips.

"I've never been in such an odd situation before, but neither does it matter. Right now, I feel that if I don't make love with you, I am going to burst. My desire for you is so strong right now that I can think of nothing else."

He quickly pulled off the rest of his clothes, sweeping her off her feet, scooping her up into his arms. Her long hair trailed over one side, her long legs over the other. "I've never been seduced this way before by a woman." He headed toward the bed.

"Think of it as an awakening of power."

He gently laid her on the bed, straddling her, reaching down to kiss her. The taste of her honeyed lips sent hot chills up his spine. Her flowery essence filled his nostrils. His body burned for this beautiful woman. Her skin was like velvet, her hair long and shiny. Her kisses set him on fire. Stone ran his hands down her bare body, then leaned over and took one nipple into his mouth.

"Oh! Oh, my," she cried, and he felt her body trembling. When he slid a hand down and around the delicious curve of her thigh, he couldn't help thinking she was like a vibrant winding river. He was going along for a ride not even caring where the current took him. All he knew was that it was going to be a sweet and satisfying journey. He took her other nipple into his mouth and her back arched up off the bed.

"I never knew this could feel so good," she said through a breathy whisper.

"You'll find that you've missed out on a lot of pleasure and enjoyment being raised by nuns," he told her.

"Then I want you to help me experience it all!"

"Slow down," he told her with a chuckle. "There is a lot you haven't experienced and we cannot do it all at one time."

"Well, I am a fast learner. Show me more. I want to feel more pleasure."

"All right," he said, kissing her behind the ear and letting his tongue enter. She giggled and pushed him away.

"That was so loud," she told him.

"Then how about this?" He continued to kiss her, letting his kisses trail down her chest, past her breasts and down her taut stomach. He was trying to go slow to seduce her, but was only driving himself crazy. He kissed her belly button, swirling his tongue down around inside. She giggled again, pushing him away.

"That is an odd place to kiss me."

"If you think that is odd, then wait until you see where I plan to go next." He waggled his eyebrows and looked down at the juncture between her legs.

"Oh," she said, realizing what he meant. "Oooooh," she said again, seeming to be thinking about it. "Mayhap you're right. We shouldn't feel all the pleasure at once."

"Or, at least, not on your first time," he agreed. "I say we save that for next time."

"I am glad to hear you suggest there will be a next time." She surprised him by raising her legs around his waist, clamping them together tightly.

When he slipped his hand between her legs, he was surprised again to find her already wet and ready. He supposed his quick act of foreplay was more than enough to excite a girl of her age who was still a virgin.

"Hurry up, Stone. I can no longer wait."

"And neither can I." He didn't waste time slipping his weapon of love inside her, causing both of them to come to life now.

"Persimmon, if I am too rough, please tell me and I will stop," he said, hoping she wouldn't make him stop since he had no idea if he could anymore. Desire filled his being and passion spurred him on.

"I want you. All of you, Stone. Please, don't deny me."

Her words gave him the permission he needed. They did the dance of love, finding the perfect rhythm between them. He held back for as long as he could. And when he heard her coos of passion turn into a louder moan of ecstasy, he knew she had found her pent-up release. It didn't take any time to find his as well. Their lovemaking made him feel alive, hot, happy and fully sated.

Rolling off of her, he flipped onto his back, pulling her atop him, wrapping his arms around her and burying his nose in her sweet, silky hair.

It was a few minutes before either of them could find the breath to speak. Then he heard her soft, sweet voice while her cheek was pressed up against his chest.

"We did it, Stone. I finally did it. We made love."

"Yes. Yes, we did." He smoothed down her hair with one hand, feeling like he never wanted this moment to end.

"Did you like it?" he had to ask.

"I loved it. Did you?"

"You have no idea."

"So, do you think it worked? Do you think it awakened the gazing crystal and that I'll be able to scry now?"

"I don't know," he told her. "But if not, I won't stop you from trying again."

They both laughed and then she sat up, pushing her long hair out of her eyes.

"I'm sorry, but I am too excited and need to know the answer right now. I can't wait a moment longer." She slid off the bed and her bare feet pitter-pattered across the floor. She hurried over to a table, picking up the gazing orb, and then heading back to him.

"Are you really going to try it? Right now?" He chuckled because she was so cute and so excited to learn. Most women he'd made love with wanted him to just lay there and talk after coupling. They didn't want him to hurry away. But this woman was unique. She seemed to be all about business. Although it surprised him, it made his feelings for her even stronger. He sat up, scooching back on the bed.

"Well, yes, I was going to try it." Her bright blue eyes flashed upward. "Why? Do you think it is insensitive to do it right now since we just made love? I mean, I suppose I could wait a little longer if you think I should."

"Don't wait on my behalf," he answered with a chuckle. "I find your enthusiasm and your innocence refreshing."

"I don't think I'm innocent anymore after that!"

"Nay, I suppose that wasn't the best word to use. Go ahead, Persimmon. I want you to try it."

"All right, then." A wide smile crossed her face. She held up the gazing orb in two hands. "What should I ask? Or should I just look into it and not ask anything at all?"

"You're asking the wrong person, sweetheart. I

don't know the first thing about magic or magical beings and neither do I pretend to know. Just do whatever you feel in your heart is the right thing to do."

"All right." She closed her eyes and took a deep breath, seeming to think. Then she slowly released the air from her mouth. "I'll try both ways," she told him. First, she just looked into the orb, and when nothing happened, she moved her face closer, focusing hard on the ball. "I don't think this way is working."

"Then try asking a question," he prompted her.

"All right, I will. Where can we find the thieves?" she asked aloud, staring once again at the gazing ball. After a few minutes and a couple more questions, the excited smile on her face disappeared and was replaced by a frown.

"It didn't work?" he asked.

"Nay." She shook her head, looking like she was about to cry.

"I'm sorry, Persimmon." Stone stood up and walked over to get his clothes. "I really hoped that would work for you."

"I was sure it would. Mayhap I did something wrong. Mayhap we should try it again?"

Stone dressed as he spoke. "As much as I'd like to stay right here and try it over and over again for the rest of the day, I'm afraid I can't. Time is of the essence. I really need to hunt down Rancor and Filip before it is too late."

"I'm sorry," she said, looking at the ground and seeming like she hated herself right now. He didn't understand it. She threw the orb down on the bed and got up and started dressing.

"Sorry for what? We both enjoyed ourselves, didn't we? So it wasn't a waste of time if that's what you're thinking."

"Nay, that's not it, Stone."

"Then why do you sound as if you're being hard on yourself?" He pulled up his breeches and tied them.

"I'm sorry for failing. For letting you down."

"Stop it!" He stopped dressing and walked over and pulled her back into his arms. She buried her face against his bare chest. "You could never let me down and I don't want to hear you say that ever again. Do you understand?"

"I want to help you. Honest, I do. I want to be able to help my family and any of the people of Mura who need it as well. But it is just not working and I don't know why."

"You can't save the world, Persimmon, and neither is it your job. Remember that."

"But bad things are going to happen and I won't be able to stop them."

"Mayhap that is so. But did you ever think that it wasn't your destiny to stop anything from happening?"

"What do you mean?" She sniffled and pulled out of his embrace.

"I mean, I have a job to do, and I suppose I was just looking for a fast and easy way to get to where I'm going. I never should have asked you to scry for me. I don't mind hard work."

"And I don't mind going with you to help you attain your goal."

"Nay," he said firmly, stepping away and pulling a tunic over his head. The he pushed into his boots and ended by strapping on his weapon belt. "It is too dangerous and I don't want anything to happen to you."

"But I have magic," she told him. "I'll be protected by it. I've already used it to help us, and I won't hesitate to do it once again."

"I said no," he told her, picking up his sword and sliding it into the scabbard. "Now stay here where you'll be safe. I will see you later." He kissed her once more, giving her a quick hug and then walked over and pulled open the door.

"Will you? Will you really return?" she asked, sounding like she was looking for validation.

He turned to see her standing there, looking so forlorn.

"Of course, I will, sweetheart. I always carry out my promises."

"And what if you find the portal open? Then, what will you do? Will you go through it?"

"Yes, I'm counting on finding it again. I have to do so in order to return to Taelgonoth and warn my king about Sethor's plans."

"But if you go back to Taelgonoth...if you go back to your homeland, you will never return to Mura. Will you?"

"Well, I—" He really hadn't thought that far ahead. His focus had been on his job and getting back home. But now after coupling with Persimmon, everything had changed. He had feelings for her and really didn't want to leave her behind. Plus, he could see that if he left, Persimmon would think he was abandoning her like everyone else in her life had done. That is the last thing he wanted her to believe. "Persimmon, I can't answer that right now. No one knows how to open or close the portal. Even if I get through it again, I might never have the chance to return to Mura if it doesn't open once again. Do you understand?"

"Then I guess this is goodbye, isn't it?" Her words stabbed into his heart like a sharp knife.

"Nay. Don't say that." He squeezed his eyes closed, feeling the pressure of being torn. He wanted to stay here with Persimmon, but also felt a calling and obligation to carry out his mission and to get back home. "We have to remain optimistic, sweetheart." He walked back to her and kissed her on the nose. "Let's not make this a goodbye. We'll just say, see you later."

Without waiting for her to respond, he turned and walked out the door. Stone made it all the way to the courtyard when Gregor Lithum rode through the gates of Kasculbough with a sense of great urgency on his face.

"Gregor is back," Rhys called out to Stone.

"I thought he went back to Macada Castle," said Aithrod as he fastened a bag to a horse that Rhys had lent them.

"He did go back," said Rhys. "If he's returned so soon, he must have information for us. It must be important."

"Let's see what he has to say." Stone hurried over with the other men to greet Gregor. "Good morning," Stone called out. Fang trailed at his side.

"I have news." Gregor hopped off the horse. A stable boy took the reins of his horse for him.

"What is it?" asked Rhys. "Is King Sethor up to something?"

"Does it have something to do with Rancor Ruse?" asked Stone.

"Yes to both," said the man. "I was able to find out information and sneak in and back out of Macada Castle without the king seeing or suspecting me."

"Do tell." Stone was anxious to know where to find his thieves.

"It seems Sethor is preparing his army." Gregor shook his head in disgust.

"For what? He wants a war with us?" Rhys frowned. "I'll contact my brothers anon."

"Nay." Gregor held up his hand. "The thieves are taking Sethor and a good sized army to a cave for some reason."

"Damn," swore Stone. "He's taking his men to the Quamm Caves, hoping to be able to go through the portal to Taelgonoth. He's going to attack King Helix and take his throne as his own."

"All those men can't possibly get through the portal before it closes, can they?" asked Aithrod. "I mean, if it even opens again at all."

"I'm sure he is counting on it," said Gregor.

"Rancor either knows how to work the portal, or has convinced the king that they can figure it out together," said Stone.

"When are they leaving?" Rhys wanted to know.

"Tomorrow at dawn," the man reported.

"How long will it take for them to get there?"

Stone asked, already weighing out the options in his head.

"It'll take a full day on horseback to get over the mountains and to the Quamm Caves," Rhys told them.

"Then we need to get there first," said Stone. "We leave at once."

"And do what?" asked Aithrod. "Stone, we can't fight against or stop an entire army."

"Mayhap not, but my brothers and I can certainly try, and at least slow them down," said Rhys. "I'll prepare my soldiers at once and send a missive to Zann to do the same."

"Won't that cause a war between you and Sethor?" asked Stone. "That is not what we want at all. I can't let you make that sacrifice, but thank you."

"Well, then what do you suggest we do to stop Sethor and his army from going through the portal and claiming Taelgonoth?" asked Rhys.

"I don't know, but I wish I did." Stone felt helpless and no longer hopeful.

"We have magic on our side. That should count for something," said a woman.

Stone turned to find Persimmon and Medea standing there listening. He hadn't even heard them approach.

"Aye, that's true." Rhys nodded. "Sethor has no defense against magic."

"No, ladies, I can't let you risk your lives this way," said Stone, wanting to protect them.

"We need to get there before Sethor," said Aithrod. "If luck is on our side and we can go back through the portal before them, we can warn King

Helix. That way, he and his soldiers can be ready if Sethor and his men do get through.”

“Good idea,” agreed Rhys.

“I can get you to the caves quickly by transporting and taking you with me,” offered Medea.

“I will come with you,” said Persimmon. “Medea and I have powers to use against Sethor and the others if need be.”

“I can contact Alaina and ask for her help as well,” added Medea.

“Nay. Persimmon, I want you and the rest of the women to stay here where you’re safe. Aithrod and I can do this alone. I don’t want anyone from Mura getting hurt on my account. This is my mission and I will see it through to the end, no matter what the outcome.”

“Well, what about you two? And Fang?” asked Persimmon, reaching down to pet the dog. “We don’t want any harm to befall any of you either.”

“That’s right,” said Medea. “Please, let us help.”

Stone looked at Aithrod, not knowing what to do.

“I say, let them try,” said Aithrod with a shrug.

“Medea does have some awesome powers,” Rhys told him.

“And I haven’t been able to use them lately, since I’ve been so busy just being a mother,” said Medea.

“Nay. I will never forgive myself if anything happens to the women. Aithrod and I only will go. If we can get back through the portal and warn our king, no one but King Sethor and his army will be at risk.” Stone knew the magical help of the women could come in handy, but the protector part of him wouldn't allow it. He didn't want women at risk, and he certainly didn't want little children to grow up without their mother if something would happen to them. "The question is, how do we even know if the portal is going to open again."

"Or where it will appear," added Rhys.

"And what about the gnomes? Don't forget about those pesky gnomes." Aithrod faked a shiver. "They are nasty and it's not going to be easy to get past them."

"Right. The gnomes," said Storm, sighing and shaking his head. "Why can't anything ever be easy?"

"Stone, you said my father was in the cave and helped you fight off the gnomes last time, right?" asked Persimmon.

"Aye. Why?"

"Mayhap he'll help again. Or, at least, he might know when and where the portal will reappear. I mean, he is a sage. He should know something."

Rhys let out a groan and Medea shot him a stern look.

"I don't even know where to find Elric," said Stone.

"That's easy." Medea stepped forward. "I can take you to his home atop the cliffs of Glint."

"Glint," repeated Stone, trying to remember what he'd heard this name before.

"Glint is the home of the elven queendom," Rhys explained. "If you are going there, you'd better take Lira with you."

"I'll get her at once." With a swish of her hand through the air, Medea transported, disappearing.

"I'm coming with you," said Gregor. "I want to

help make those thieves who killed my parents pay for what they have done."

"I'm coming, too," said Rhys. "As a king of Mura, it is my job to protect all of you, and I will not let you change my mind."

"Then, I shall not even try," answered Stone. "All right. Let's get ready and hope for the best. But this mission will be with the men only, and that is my final decision." Stone turned to make his way back to load his horse.

"Stone, wait." Persimmon ran after him. "Please, let me help too."

"I appreciate the offer, but I can't let you risk your life," said Stone, stopping in his tracks and turning to take her hands in his. "Please, stay here. If you come along, I'll just be distracted, trying to look out for your safety."

"But I have powers that can help you."

"Can you look into your gazing orb and tell me when and where the portal will appear again?" he asked.

"Well, no." She shook her head and looked down at the ground. "Not yet, anyway."

"Then there is no reason for you to come with us. Stay here inside the castle walls where you will be safe." He continued to walk.

"Stone Nightstalker, you are acting recklessly. You need the help of magic and you know it. The more, the better. You will never be able to collect Rancor and Filip as well as hold off an entire army by yourself."

"I won't be alone." He fastened a bag of food to the horse as he spoke. "I'll have Aithrod and Fang with me. Fang barked as if he agreed. "And Rhys and Gregor will be there as well."

"What about the women?" she asked. "The ones with the true powers?"

He slowly looked back at her and ran his hand lovingly against her cheek. "Persimmon, if anything ever happened to you I could never forgive myself. You need to understand this."

"Nothing is going to happen to me. Now let me come along and help."

"You can accompany me to see your father, but after that, I proceed without you. Do you understand?"

"I understand that you are being foolish, Stone. Or perhaps proud. Either way, you are going to have to accept the help of women if you want to succeed."

"We'll see," he said, still not willing to let her or the other women risk their lives on his mission. "We'll see."

* * *

"Hold on tight." Persimmon grabbed one of Medea's hands, while Stone took the other, getting ready to transport.

"What about the horses?" asked Stone.

"I can only transport two at a time," explained Medea. "I will come back for them and also the others. But for now, we need to get the two of you to Elric. I will bring Lira next."

"All right. I'm ready." Persimmon closed her eyes, squeezing Medea's hand, not sure what to expect.

"I hope this won't be as terrifying as when Alaina

whipped us through the air and—" Stone's words were cut off as a vibrating sound filled Persimmon's ears. Then her stomach became queasy and she felt a surge of energy bolt through her. With a sharp wind against her face, her body got lighter and lighter until she wasn't even sure she was on the ground anymore. Curious, she opened her eyes to peek out and screamed. A blur of mountains below her was so far down that she almost had the feeling she had left this earth. Then, as fast as it started, it all stopped with a thump. Her feet hit the ground and she stumbled, thrusting forward, but Stone reached out to catch her.

"Whoa, there," he said to her, almost sounding as if he were speaking to a horse.

"You'll get used to it after the first few times," said Medea with a big smile from ear to ear. "Do you want me to transport you all the way up the cliff to Elric's house as well?"

"No. No more," Persimmon answered with her hand on her stomach. She looked to where Medea pointed. Sure enough, a small cabin sat way up high, atop a pinnacle cliff. To the left of her was a big green castle that she was sure must be the Elven Queendom. To the right was a lake with a bridge leading to an area with a lot of quaint little colorful houses.

"Is that where the elves live?" she asked.

"Nay, that is the land of the Fae," explained Medea. To your left is Castle Glint, and behind you are the homes of the elves."

She slowly turned to see a bunch of cute little dwellings. Each one had a hedge of bushes surrounding it, as if it were done for protection of some sort or perhaps privacy.

"You look a little pale, and like you don't feel well," surmised Stone. "I think it's best if we hike up the mountain on foot to see Elric, but thank you for the offer, Medea."

"Yes. I agree." Persimmon wasn't up for another of Medea's transporting trips just yet.

"All right. I'll be back soon with Lira," Medea told them. "I will get your horses, too. Do you want me to bring Rhys and the others here or drop them off at the cave?"

"Mayhap at the cave will be better so they can keep an eye open for Rancor and Sethor," suggested Stone.

"And watch for the portal to open as well," Persimmon quickly added.

"All right. Good luck with Elric." With a wave of her hand, Medea disappeared.

"My, people come and go so quickly here on Mura," said Persimmon.

"Don't they do that on Lornoon too?" questioned Stone.

"I'm not sure. But in the convent, everyone moved slowly."

"I still can't believe you grew up in a convent." Stone shook his head. "So you never practiced your magic? I mean, moving things with your mind."

"Nay, not around anyone. It was forbidden. I only practiced in my room when no one was watching. Or on my trips home to see my mother."

"Your relationship with your mother seems odd," Stone continued. "I mean, my family was close when

I was growing up. But yours seems so...I mean they seem to..."

"Shun me," she finished his sentence for him. "It's all right to say it aloud since it is the truth. And before you ask, I really don't know why my parents did that. I am also sorry that Elric stole your king's gemstones. I have always been told by my mother that the man is greedy."

"I'm not surprised," said Stone as they walked. "Taelgonoth is filled with greedy people, too."

"So your homeland sounds like a place with lots of bad people. Is your king like King Sethor? Bad, too?"

"Not necessarily bad, but greedy and demanding. Honestly, I can't seem to find anyone I trust on Taelgonoth anymore. Except for Aithrod and Fang."

"Really?" Persimmon held up the hem of her gown and took a step over a puddle. "Then why do you work for such a man?"

He shrugged. "I have no choice. I need to earn a living to survive. King Helix holds power and with that power comes my protection."

"Protection? I don't understand. From whom?"

"From everyone, sweetheart. I am telling you, my land is a dark place to be right now. I was hoping if I can catch and bring in more thieves and murderers for persecution, mayhap the king will set things right again. The way they used to be when my father was alive and helping out the king."

"And by bringing him back his jewels, you're going to create more of an alliance with him. Right?"

"It can't hurt."

"Plus, you'll marry his daughter," she said sadly. "That will give you the protection you crave as well."

Stone didn't answer.

"Are the gems really your king's? Or did he steal them from someone else? My father claims they belong to him."

"I don't know, and honestly, I don't care," Stone told her.

"You didn't even try to find out?" she asked in shock.

"In my line of work, you have to be careful what kind of questions you ask."

"I see." She didn't really see, but was hesitant to pursue this right now.

"We need to walk faster." He held out his hand and she took it.

Looking up the steep mountain it felt like they were never going to get to the top by Elric's house. "Are we really going to hike all the way up there?"

"You didn't want Medea's help, so yes, we have to walk. Don't worry, I'll help you. It'll be fine. Come on, let's go." Stone held her hand tightly and together they briskly followed the trail leading almost straight up, to Elric's home.

"Mayhap we should wait for Lira," suggested Persimmon, breathing heavier, the higher they got. "After all, she has a much better relationship with Elric than I do."

"Mayhap it is time you change that," Stone said as he moved in front of her and continued to climb.

"I cannot change something when I don't know why it even exists in the first place." She kept her eyes on the ground, not wanting to fall off the side of the mountain.

"Just ask him."

"What?"

Stone stopped and turned to face her. "Ask Elric why he acts like he hates you. He doesn't seem like the kind of man who bites his tongue, so I am sure he'll tell you what is on his mind if you inquire."

"I'm not certain I can do that."

"Of course, you can. And I'll be right there with you." He held out his hand again and she willingly took it. Mayhap with Stone at her side she would have the courage and strength to face Elric and finally find out the secrets of the past.

They finally made it up to Elric's dwelling. Stone made a fist and rapped upon the door.

"Who's bothering me?" came Elric's grumpy shout from within.

"You'd better say something," whispered Stone. "If he knows it's me, he's likely to push us down the mountain."

"Me?" Her hand went to her chest. "Are you forgetting he doesn't like me?"

"He called me a big oaf and a fool. You are of his blood so we have a better chance if it's you instead of me."

"Fine." She let out a deep sigh. "Father, it's me," she called out. "Please, let me in."

"Lira?" The door swung open and the elf's face appeared. "Oh, it's you and the big oaf. Go away, I'm busy." Elric tried to close the door on them, but Stone stuck his foot in the threshold and stopped him.

"Let us in, Elric." Stone wasn't going to back down.

"Nay! You are not getting the gemstones, so you might as well leave right now." He clutched the bag of gems to his chest

"Do you ever put them down?" mumbled Stone.

"Father, we just walked all the way up the mountain to see you. We want to talk. Please, don't turn us away." Persimmon tried her best to convince Elric to let them enter.

"If I let you in, the big oaf needs to promise he is not going to try again to take my gemstones away from me."

"You mean King Helix of Taelgonoth's gems," Stone corrected him. "Jewels that you stole."

"Stone, please." Persimmon laid a hand on his arm and willed him to be quiet. "If you put him on his defense, we are never going to get inside."

"You're right. I'm sorry," said Stone. "Can we please come in, Elric?"

"You promise me, first." The elf was a stubborn little thing. He was also so different from Persimmon's mother that Persimmon wondered how in the world the two of them ever got together in the first place and how she was even born.

"Stone. Please." Persimmon looked at him and raised a brow.

"Fine. I promise," he groaned, shaking his head as soon as Elric turned around.

"All right. Come in and close the door."

Persimmon entered her father's house, stopping to look around and take in her surroundings. It was tiny. All the furniture was small, like it was made for a child. She supposed it was because Elric himself wasn't taller than a child.

"Sit down, sit down." Elric zipped over to the open window, closing the shutter quickly. "Did Queen Sasha see you come here?" he asked, with one eye squinted. He darted over and climbed up on the table to be the same height as them. "She did, didn't she?" He acted as if it worried him that the elven queen might have even seen them.

"Who?" asked Persimmon, knowing the answer but stalling for time to work up her courage. She checked out each of the chairs and finally chose one to sit on.

"Lira's aunt," spat Elric. "She is queen of Glint now since your sister foolishly gave up the throne and the queendom to go rule with that shapeshifting husband of hers. What a waste, I swear."

"Father, that's not a nice thing to say," scolded Persimmon.

"Zann is a shapeshifter?" asked Stone in surprise, still standing.

"Yes. I'm surprised you even know what it means." Elric raised his chin and proceeded to look down his nose at Stone. "After all, you are naught but a helpless human since you have no magic in your land and hold no power in the least."

"Of course, I know what it means. And I'm sorry to have disappointed you with my mundane abilities. So, tell me. What does Zann shift into? And how often does it occur?"

"Not that it's any of your business, but Zann can turn into a man-eating white wolf at any moment.

You'd better beware," snapped Elric, his arms flaying around above his head like a madman.

"Man-eating?" repeated Stone.

"Father! That is a lie. How can you even say that?" Lira stood in the open doorway. "My husband can shift into a wolf, that part is true. However, he has never eaten a human, I assure you." Lira entered the room.

"Lira? You're here, too? Who did you bring with you?" In a blur, the elf sped over to the door, looked out in both directions and then slammed the door.

"I'm by myself, Father." Lira walked over and sat down on a small chair. "Why are you so worried?"

"I don't want any of you bringing those thieves to my door." Elric zipped back to the window and paced the floor.

"Oh, you mean the thieves that you stole the gems from in the first place?" asked Stone. "Speaking of that, did you take them all from Rancor or does he have any left? Either way, I'll need you to hand them over to me now." Stone's hand shot out, his open palm waiting for the stones. He still stood instead of sitting in the chairs that were much too small for a normal sized man.

"I told you, I didn't steal anything," spat Elric, moving closer to Stone. "I found them on the floor of the cave. The stupid thieves were so busy fighting off the gnomes, they didn't even see me there." He clutched the bag at his side.

"Do they have some gemstones left?" asked Stone. "The king didn't tell me how many went missing."

"How should I know?" Elric bit at a hangnail.

"They are so stupid, even if they did have more, they have probably lost them by now. Besides, these are of no use to humans."

"What do you mean, Father?" asked Persimmon.

"You know something about these gems that you aren't telling us," Stone accused him.

"Why do you think that?" asked Persimmon.

"I can read people and their reactions. Elric wouldn't look at me when I asked how many stones there were and he bit at his finger nervously," said Stone. "That proves to me he knows more than he is letting on."

"Do you, Father?" asked Lira. "Do you know something about these gemstones?"

"Never mind that," spat Elric. "Stone promised he wouldn't try to get them from me and he broke his promise. I can't trust you, Stonestealer." He stopped and folded his arms over his chest. One eyebrow raised in the air as he perused Stone.

"Me? You can't trust me?" asked Stone, slapping his chest with his opposite palm. "How about I can't trust you?"

"Stone, please," Persimmon said softly, not wanting trouble. "You did promise."

Stone shook his head, let out a sigh and slowly lowered his hand to his side. "They must still have some of King Helix's gems. They have to. If not, how did they manage to convince King Sethor into following them to a portal and taking over the kingdom of Taelgonoth?"

"I agree with Stone," said Lira. "King Sethor is a greedy man. He wouldn't believe Rancor if bait hadn't been dangled in front of his nose to lure him into doing anything."

"Why does this man Rancor and his counterpart want to take over Taelgonoth?" asked Persimmon, still trying to understand about Stone's land.

"There is only one king where I live," explained Stone. "And that king rules everyone and everything. I suppose Rancor thinks if he can lure another king and his army there to seize it, that he'll somehow be in a good position."

"Father, do you really think if this transpires that Sethor would give Rancor a position at court?" asked Lira.

"How should I know?" Elric ground out, climbing atop a chair and thumping his fingers against the table. "And why are all of you wasting my precious time? I told you I'm not turning over the stones, so get lost."

"He's holding back on us again," said Stone. "See the way he nervously raps his fingers on the table?"

Elric quickly folded his arms and stuck his hands under his armpits.

"We're here for another reason as well," Persimmon told him. "We had hoped since you're a sage, you would be able to tell us when the portal will open, or how to open or close it on our own."

"What?" Elric squinted, making a face and slowly turned toward Persimmon. "Why would you be asking me that when you have the ability to see the future in the gazing orb?"

"I don't have that ability, Father. I tried but haven't been able to achieve it."

"Ah, I see." His focus was on Stone next. "So, I'm

guessing you coupled with the big oaf, telling him it would fire up the gazing crystal but it didn't, did it? It is the same thing your mother did to me all those years ago. She lured me to her bed just to use me."

"Hah!" spat Stone. "I hardly think you'd let anyone use you if you weren't getting something out of it."

Persimmon didn't like Elric referring to her mother in such a way. She also didn't like the fact her father called Stone an oaf or that he knew she made love to Stone. She wasn't sure if he had been listening at her door or if his abilities of being a sage led him on to their secret.

"Father, Stone and I didn't—" Persimmon heard Stone clear his throat and she stopped in midsentence. When she looked over at him, he nodded at her father. She realized the right thing to do was to be honest. "All right. Yes, we did make love but I thought it would work to unleash the powers of the gazing orb. After Stone kissed me I saw colors in the orb. I supposed coupling would give me the ability to scry since by kissing it brought about colors. I never meant to use him in the way that you are suggesting." She looked at Stone. "I mean, it was warranted by both of us. I think."

"Hah! So you did use him. And in his lustful manner he allowed it," said Elric.

"Don't speak for me, Elric," grunted Stone. "She did nothing wrong. She told me her suspicions and I went along with it by my own choice."

"Father, I only want to help others, but sadly, it seems that I still cannot scry."

"But you knew about the old couple on the

road," said Lira. "Certainly you have some ability to see the future."

"I never saw the vision in the gazing orb. I just felt it, I guess. But I assure you, I never saw a thing in the gazing ball until I arrived in Mura and Stone entered my life. Now, I have seen swirling colors and I also saw Fang struggling in the water. I am so close to making it work." She looked over at her father. "So, was the reason I was born because Mother tried to access her powers to scry as well?"

"It was," Elric answered. "I am sorry to say I truly had feelings for your mother, but she had none for me. She knew I was an elf and a sage and thought she needed a magical mate in order to make it work."

"But Stone isn't magical." Persimmon looked over at him. "I suppose that's why it didn't work."

Lira cleared her throat. "Father, you tricked Zann and I into getting married, telling me that I'd regain my lost powers by making love to him. That didn't work either."

"I only did that to help you regain your confidence. I also knew you needed a father for your daughter to replace the husband you lost. Zann seemed like the most likely one to fill that position, even if he wasn't my first choice."

"If I wasn't happy about the outcome, I'd be furious at you right now," said Lira. "But Zann and I fell in love and I am happy with the way things turned out."

"Hmph!" grunted Elric. "Persimmon, didn't your mother ever explain anything to you?"

"About my powers?" asked Persimmon.

"Nay. About why she never married me, and why you had to grow up in a convent."

"No, she didn't," said Persimmon, wanting answers. "I would like to know why. I would also like to know why you seem so bitter toward me."

"Yes, Father, I would like to know that as well," chimed in Lira. "You've not been very kind to Persimmon since she's arrived."

"Luna put you in a convent to protect you from the evils that could befall you."

"What evils? From scrying if I was able to activate the orb? But it wasn't even mine at the time."

"Probably that, too, but it's not what I meant," said Elric. "You see, I wasn't the first man she made love to," he explained. "She was in love with a mere human who happened to come through a portal."

"Really? Mother never told me that."

"Wait a minute. What portal?" asked Stone. "And who was this man?"

"They made love and the man stole something from me and then disappeared. That's when your mother coupled with me, desperate to be able to use the orb to find her lover again."

"So just like Persimmon, she believed that coupling would bring her scrying power through the orb?" asked Lira.

"Yes. I don't know where witches get these silly ideas." Elric rolled his eyes.

"If that is not what activated the orb and gave her the power to scry, then what was?" asked Persimmon.

"Dang, if I know." Elric zipped around the room, picking up items and dusting with his sleeve.

"I thought you are a sage," said Stone. "Shouldn't you know things like that?"

Elric returned and jumped up to sit on the table in front of Persimmon. "When it comes to the gods and why they do things or how things work, I am at a loss. But ask me about elves or the fae and I can tell you anything you want to know."

"Who said anything about gods?" asked Stone.

"Huh?" Elric looked as if he'd slipped up and told them something he shouldn't. "I don't know what you mean."

"What I want to know, is who was the other man who made love with Mother?" asked Persimmon.

"Yes, I would like to know that, too," said Stone with interest.

"It was King Kapion," said Elric.

"Who?" asked Persimmon.

"Oh, nay. It was King Helix Kapion of Taelgonoth," said Stone. "My king, wasn't it? And you are saying he stole those gemstones from you? Now, why don't I believe that is the whole story?"

"It's true!" cried Elric. "I got those stones from the gods. They are magical. That is why he wanted them."

"Ah, now we're getting somewhere. So, we're back to the gods again, are we?" asked Stone.

"How did the king even know those rocks held magic?" asked Lira.

Elric shrugged and made a face. "Well, I might have bragged a little about them to Luna. Trying to attract your mother's interest," he said, looking at Persimmon. "You see, she must have either told him about it, or he overheard." Elric bit at his hangnail again.

"Father, did you steal those stones from the gods? Is that why they've frowned upon you lately?" asked Persimmon.

"I might have." Elric looked over at them and rolled his eyes again. "Oh, all right, so yes, I stole them. And the gods are going to take away my elven powers if I don't return all thirteen stones soon. I have managed to keep it a secret that the stones are gone for over twenty-five years but they finally noticed and now I am in serious trouble," admitted Elric.

"So, you're saying those stones really belong to the gods of Mura and King Helix stole them from you over twenty-five years ago?" asked Stone in disbelief.

"Yes, that is exactly what I'm saying." Elric sighed. "I kept distracting the gods every time they asked about the stones and was able to hold them off. I mean, it's not like they needed those stones and powers anyway. Then, luck finally came my way. I was near the Quamm Caves recently and I heard something happening inside. That's when I discovered the portal, the thieves, and my stolen gemstones."

"The gods' gemstones," Lira corrected him.

"Whatever." So when the portal appeared in the cave and I found the stones, I was elated. There were thirteen stones in all, but I only found eleven. I need the last two before I can approach the gods to return them."

"And that's why you want the one I have," said Stone with a nod.

"So hand it over," demanded Elric. "You know now that the gemstones are not your king's so there is no need for you to bring them back to him."

"Not so fast," said Stone. "Even if I give you the one I have, you have one more to find. My guess is that Rancor has it. And you're going to need me to track him down to get it for you."

"Never mind the stones. Elric, are you really my father? Or is King Helix Kapion the man who sired me?" asked Persimmon, starting to understand her father's bitter attitude toward her now.

"I don't know," said Elric, shaking his head. "I'm not sure your mother really knew either."

"Then I need to find out on my own."

"No!" both Elric and Stone said together.

"It's too dangerous, Persimmon." Stone held concern in his voice.

"The man is evil. Why would you even want to know if he is the one who sired you?" asked Elric.

"Mayhap, because I have not had a real father my entire life and I would like to finally have one." Grief filled her heart. She didn't want to be the daughter of an evil man, but neither did she want an elven father who had ignored her and seemed to despise her for the last twenty-five years, even though it was no fault of hers. She was torn, but felt the burning desire to know the truth once and for all.

"Once I finally convinced Luna how bad King Kapion was, she decided she would have to hide you, Persimmon. Because if the portal ever opened again and he came back, she wasn't sure he wouldn't try to kidnap you, wanting to claim you as his daughter and take you away from her. It was only a matter of time before he figured out how powerful you would be."

"Oh," she answered. "Everything makes sense now. Mayhap that is why I don't look like you and have pointy ears."

"So she might not even be half-elf after all," Stone spoke up. "For all we know, she might be half-human."

"That's right," said Persimmon. "What if I am really the daughter of the King of Taelgonoth? Then what?"

"Don't say that! Ever!" spat Elric. "You are half elf. Everyone knows that."

"Do we?" asked Persimmon, seeming to upset her father.

When Elric got off the table quickly, one of the gemstones fell from his pouch. Persimmon was attracted to it. She slowly reached out to pick it up.

"Father, I don't understand," said Persimmon, closing her fingers around the gemstone. "Why didn't you or Mother ever tell me any of this?"

"Some things are better off left unsaid," replied Elric.

"Is that really true?" asked Persimmon, feeling her heart sink. She rubbed her thumb over the stone. "If only one of you would have told me all this years ago, I wouldn't have had to feel so abandoned my entire life."

"You weren't abandoned. It was done for your own protection." Elric slammed his hand down on the table.

Persimmon felt the stone become so hot in her hand that she had to throw it down in front of her.

"Ow!" she cried, rubbing her fingers together, trying to stop the pain. She saw a ghostly figure at the far side of the room and knew immediately who it was. "Mother," she gasped. "Why didn't you tell me?"

Be careful, Persimmon. Now that you know these things, you are in more danger than you believe.

"Luna is here?" Elric spun around in a fast circle, looking in every direction. "Where is she? Why can't I see her? Luna, where are you and what do you want?"

"She's right there." Persimmon pointed to the ghost of her mother. "She's warning me to be careful."

"She's speaking? What is she saying? I need to know." Elric was visibly upset.

"Why do you need to know?" asked Persimmon. "Are you afraid she might tell me something else that you've been keeping from me?"

"Uh, excuse me," said Stone. His eyes were focused on the table and his jaw dropped. "Did anyone else see that? Persimmon touched a gemstone and it is glowing." Stone scooped up the stone.

"Be careful! It's hot," warned Persimmon.

"Nay, it's not. It's cold." Stone tossed it up and down in his palm. It no longer glowed.

"What?" Elric spun around. His hand slapped against the pouch at his side. "How did you get that? Give it to me." He sped over to Stone in a blur, but Stone was ready for him. He closed his fingers tightly over the gem.

"Not so fast, little man." Stone chuckled and held out his finger, pointing at him. "Tell us the truth. These gemstones hold great power. Power that you know is somehow connected to Persimmon.

That is why you want to keep them from my king, and why King Kapion would have wanted to take Persimmon if he'd ever come back. And for some strange reason, you want to keep these stones away from Persimmon as well. You have ill intentions, admit it. I'll bet you were the one who used Luna for your own purposes. It wasn't the other way around at all, was it?"

"The gemstones are from the gods, I swear it," said Elric, sounding extremely agitated now.

"Yes, we know that part," said Stone. "You stole them and are trying not to be punished."

"It is true that they hold great power?" asked Lira.

"It's power that can only be used by a chosen one," said Elric.

"Chosen one?" asked Persimmon. "Are you saying I was chosen by your gods for something?"

Elric scrunched up his face, fastened the bag of gems to his waist and looked the other way.

Elric wanted to be chosen, said her mother. *He wanted that power for himself,* Luna told her. *You weren't old enough to handle the power before so it didn't matter that you didn't have the stones. But you are of age now, daughter.*

"Mother, who is my true father?" asked Persimmon, needing to know.

I can't tell you that. And now I must leave you. Forever.

"Nay, don't leave," Persimmon begged her. "I need you."

I am sorry I abandoned you, but you have Stone Nightstalker to look after you now. He will make you happy, Persimmon. You deserve it. Don't lose him.

"Wait, Mother. I need to know how to be able to use the gazing orb. How did you do it?"

That is something you will need to find out for yourself. Goodbye, my dear. I love you.

"Nay, Mother, don't leave."

"What's happening?" asked Elric. "Where is she going? What did she say?"

"She's gone," Persimmon answered with a deep sigh. Even though her mother's ghost had frightened her before, this time it seemed to calm her and make her feel better.

"Persimmon? Who did she say was your father?" asked Stone, reaching out and placing his hand over hers.

"She said she couldn't tell me. I am not sure if she knew or not, but I intend to find out that answer on my own."

"What are you saying?" snapped Elric. "How do you think you are going to get that answer when I don't even know?"

"I need to meet King Kapion and determine for myself if he or you are my true father."

"Don't be silly," said the elf. "You don't want to go anywhere near that evil man. And please don't even think of giving him the gemstones. He can't use the powers so they are no good to him."

"Nay, but I can use them," said Persimmon, feeling her heart beat faster. "And if King Kapion is my father, he needs to know that I am a chosen one of your gods."

"This is a bad idea. Really bad." Elric paced back and forth and rubbed his hands through his hair.

"Elric," said Stone. "What I don't understand, is

how did you even get an opportunity to steal the stones from the gods in the first place?"

"My father is a messenger of the gods and goddesses of Mura," explained Lira.

"What? Nay. That's a jest, right?" Stone chuckled.

"It's true," said the elf. "The gods are also the ones who made me a sage."

"You're a messenger of the gods?" Stone shook his head, still unable to believe it.

"Sometimes, they give my father gifts," said Lira.

"They gave me that gazing ball, Persimmon." Elric nodded to her pouch.

"Not much of a gift if they knew he couldn't use it," Stone snorted.

"Did you give the gazing orb to Mother?" asked Persimmon.

"I did," the elf admitted. "I had hoped to win her over."

"You sound as if you really cared for her." This surprised Persimmon. I think Mother cared for you as well."

"I doubt it," snapped the elf.

"She never said she hated you or anything. She just called you greedy and selfish and said you can't be trusted," continued Persimmon.

"That's nothing that the rest of us don't already know," mumbled Stone.

"She even told me once that she had wished you'd stayed with us and not left us." Persimmon waited for her father's reaction.

"Too late now, isn't it?" Elric was a real grouch and it was so hard to read him.

"The gods often get angry or aggravated with my father," explained Lira.

"Gee, I can't imagine why," said Stone flippantly.

"The gifts are not always what he hopes they will be," Lira continued.

"They aggravate me just as much at times." Elric hurried over to an iron stove and put a kettle of water on the grate and lit a fire underneath it. "I just needed to know the future, and the gods wouldn't tell me. I persisted to know, and they gave me a scrying orb that only a magical witch woman could use. I didn't appreciate that gesture at all."

"Mother's ghost just told me you wanted to be the chosen one," Persimmon told Elric. "Why?"

"Why not?" he answered. "I'm a sage and people expect me to know things all the time. It is exhausting."

"Father, is something going to happen to Persimmon now that all of this is out in the open?" asked Lira, reaching out and taking hold of Persimmon's hand. "I just met my sister. I don't want to lose her."

"I don't know," said Elric, jumping in surprise when the kettle on the stove started to whistle. He sped around the room, placing a cup and saucer in front of each of them. Then he hurried over to the kettle and dropped some leaves inside and closed the lid. "If I had someone to scry for me, then I'd know these blasted things," mumbled the elf.

"Locking me away for an entire lifetime isn't going to change the future," said Persimmon. "And it still doesn't explain why you hate me so much."

"I don't hate you!" shouted the elf. "It's just been hard for me because I'm not sure...I don't know if..."

"If you're my father," Persimmon finished the sentence for him.

"Well, now you know." Elric zipped over to the stove and returned and poured them all a cup of tea.

Persimmon felt more confused and also lonelier than ever now. She cradled her cup, feeling as if she didn't really know either of her parents. "How would you use the stones if you had the power, Father?"

Elric let out a sigh. "Well, I'm not sure. First, I'd have to find out what each stone could do."

"Interesting," said Persimmon. Her gaze traveled over to Stone who now held two of the gems.

There came a knock at the door and the elf zipped over and held his hand on the door, speaking through it. "Who is it and what do you want?"

"Father, open the door and you'll find out." Lira got up and walked over to do it.

"Nay! I don't open my door unless I know who it is."

"Too bad you can't scry or you'd know," said Stone with a chuckle, picking up the small tea cup, trying to balance it on the saucer in his other hand.

"Father, I've never seen you act like this before. You are usually so fearless. Now, stop it." Lira opened the door.

"I was told Stone was here?" Aithrod stood in the doorway, breathing heavily from having climbed the path of the mountain leading to Elric's door. Fang was with him. The dog saw Stone and barked happily, knocking down Elric as he bounded into the room to be with his master. Fang jumped on Stone and Stone dropped the tea cup, sending it shattering to the floor.

"Get that monster out of here!" Elric pointed to the door, while he lie prone on the floor.

"Get down, boy." Stone petted the dog and it calmed right down. "What is it, Aithrod?"

"King Sethor and his army are on the move," Aithrod reported. "They are already nearing the Quamm Caves."

"They're not getting my gemstones," said Elric, standing up, brushing off the bag attached to his waist.

"Father, we need you," said Persimmon, hurrying to the door. "Can you tell us when the portal will appear again?"

"I don't know," said Elric with a shrug. "Portals are funny things. It's hard to control them." He zipped over to the table, clearing the tea cups, and in a blur had the broken cup from the floor cleaned up as well.

Fang's head shot back and forth and he whimpered, not able to keep an eye on the man's quick movements.

"Yes, he's right," said Lira. "We've only seen three portals here on Mura so far, but each of them has caused us many problems and heartaches."

"Who would know how to open the portal?" Stone asked Elric. "We need to access it before Sethor gets to the caves. We have to warn King Helix that they're coming before it's too late."

"King Kapion isn't going to like this," said Aithrod. "It could be the end for him."

"He's a thief. He deserves to die." Elric crossed his arms over his chest yet again.

"Then do you deserve to die, too?" asked Stone.

"Because as I see it, you are nothing but a thief as well."

"I don't know how to open the portal, but I think I might be able to direct you to someone who can do it," Elric told them.

"Who?" asked Stone.

"Before I tell you, I want to know something. Are you going to give me those two stones back and also help me get the last stone from that thief, Rancor or not?"

"I have my orders from our king," said Stone.

"Stone, please." Persimmon put her hand on his arm. "Now that we know the truth about the stones, you're not really going to give them back to your king, are you? You heard my father. Only the Chosen One can use them."

"Those gemstones are worth a lot of money," said Aithrod. "Stone, what's going on here?"

"The gemstones, I found out, were stolen by our king from Elric," Stone explained. "Elric took them from the gods of Mura first. I guess only the Chosen One by the gods can use them."

"Chosen One? Who is that?" asked Aithrod.

"The Chosen One is the same person who can open that portal," Elric explained. "It is you, Persimmon."

Fourteen

Stone, Persimmon, and the others stood just outside the Quamm Caves, thankfully having gotten there before King Sethor and his army of men arrived.

"I will distract the gnomes while the rest of you go with Persimmon to open the portal," said Elric. "Stone, go through and warn your king, but first give me the two gemstones you hold since we don't want that evil man to get them." His hand was out in front of Stone once again.

"I can't do that," said Stone.

"Persimmon will need to use one of them to try to open the portal," Elric continued.

"Will it really work, Father?" asked Lira excitedly. "Will Persimmon be able to use a stone to open a portal?"

"She will," said Elric. "One of the thirteen gems will open the portal, and also close it."

"How do you know this? I thought you said you didn't know what powers the stones held." Stone exchanged glances with Aithrod as Fang sniffed around the opening of the cave, afraid to go in since the dog remembered about the gnomes only too well.

"I might know a little about this, after all. I'm a sage, remember. I'm the keeper of knowledge."

"Do you know what each of the thirteen gemstones does?" asked Persimmon.

"Nope. Just the one." The damn elf was biting at his hangnail again.

"He's lying," said Stone.

"Father!" scolded Lira.

"Oh, all right. Yes, I do know. I found out what powers the stones have when I was guarding them for the gods. I just don't know which stone does what. Now, if only I had known it took the Chosen One to actually use them, I never would have stolen them to begin with."

"Stone, give me the one to hold that burned my hand," said Persimmon. "I already know I have a connection with that one, so mayhap it'll open the portal."

"I don't like this." Stone felt overly cautious. "We need to have a plan. And I need to bring back Rancor and Filip. I'm afraid we're not going to have time to go through the portal and return before Sethor gets here."

"Then we can hide and jump out and surprise them when they arrive," said Aithrod. "If Persimmon manages to open the portal it will attract them, so they won't be looking for us."

"Yes," said Stone. "We can grab the thieves and dive through the portal before anyone realizes what happened."

"Then, I can close the portal before King Sethor

and his armed men go through," added Persimmon with a nod.

"Wait a minute. Stop." Stone held up his hand. "We are getting ahead of ourselves. We don't even know yet if you can open the portal, sweetheart."

"I can do it. I'm sure I can. But I'll need to try all of the stones to figure out which one works on the portal."

"You heard her. She needs all of the gemstones, Elric." Stone nodded at the elf. "Give her the bag."

"Yes, Father, give me the bag of gems." Persimmon held out her hand this time.

"What? Nay!" shouted the elf, his hand going to the bag to protect it.

"Father, she is your daughter," said Lira. "You can trust her."

"I have to bring these stones back to the gods. I don't want her giving them to the big oaf."

"Trust me," said Persimmon. "I don't want the stones getting into the hands of an evil king. I just want to start trying them all before Sethor arrives."

"You can stay right here with her to guard them," Stone assured him.

"Well...all right." Finally, Elric handed over the bag of gemstones to Persimmon.

"And now yours, Stone." Persimmon held out her hand to him now.

Stone knew he had to give them up. If he didn't, Elric would probably take his back and they'd be right where they started. They were wasting precious time. And as much as he realized that he couldn't give the gems back to King Helix anymore, he also knew that if he didn't, he'd be giving up a wife, a position at

court, and most of all his security back on Taelgonoth. It was a bitter poison either way.

"Here, take them," he said, dropping them into
Persimmon's hand. "But if and when that portal
opens, I want you far from it, Persimmon. Do you
understand? Aithrod and I will pull Rancor and Filip
through it and then you close it fast behind us before
Sethor and his army can get through."

"How will I know when to open it again so you
can come back?" she asked.

"You're not going to do that," said Stone sadly,
the words breaking his heart, but it was something
that needed to be done. "Once we're through, do not
ever open the portal to Taelgonoth again. I mean it,
Persimmon."

"What are you saying?" asked Persimmon, taking the
gems from Stone. "If I don't open the portal again,
how will you return?"

"We're staying there and not returning," said
Stone, nodding at Aithrod. "Taelgonoth is our home,
not Mura. You belong here."

"Nay, I don't belong here," she said. "Stone, I
don't want you to leave me."

"Here comes Zann and his brothers," announced
Lira, taking their attention.

"They're coming," shouted Rhys, riding faster
than his brothers atop his war horse.

"Hurry, Persimmon. You've got to learn how to
open the portal quickly. Aithrod, let's get into position to surprise them." Stone gave her a kiss on the

forehead, and ran off to hide with Aithrod. Fang followed.

"You're going to have to go inside the cave to do it," Elric told her. "You need to be where the portal opened last time to make sure you're not opening a different portal entirely."

"Inside the cave?" asked Persimmon. "But I thought there were nasty gnomes in there."

"There are," said Lira. "Father, how will we hold them back?"

"Leave that to me." Elric zipped away, and returned riding on the back of Fang. Fang barked and tried to buck him off but without success.

"Let's go. Follow me," shouted the elf, leading the way inside the cave from the back of the dog.

As promised, Elric distracted the gnomes, which gave Persimmon and Lira the chance to get inside the cave without being noticed or attacked.

"Over there," yelled Elric, pointing to where the portal had appeared last time. Then, he took off once again atop Fang, with all the gnomes chasing him with their picks and axes pointed at them.

"I hope they don't get hurt," said Persimmon, pulling the first stone out of the pouch. She had added Stone's gems to the bag along with those that her father held.

"I think they'll be fine," Lira told her. "Quickly, I hear King Sethor and his army approaching. Try the gems."

The first gemstone she held did nothing to open the portal, but she screamed when her feet left the ground and she started to float around the cave.

"Oh, my!" exclaimed Lira. "Put it down and try another one. Quickly."

She slipped the first stone into her pocket and pulled another out of the bag. The next one she picked up seemed to do nothing either so she put it back and tried three more. Still, no portal appeared. "I don't understand it," said Persimmon. "None of these gems are doing anything."

"Don't be so sure about that." Lira nodded and Persimmon turned around to find a huge pile of food and several barrels of what looked like wine behind her. The gnomes spotted it and were all over it, climbing to the top of the stack.

"Well, at least we know we won't go hungry or thirsty."

"Fast, try a few more," urged Lira.

"I will." She picked up another one and it glowed pink. "How pretty," said Persimmon, getting lost in the colors of the stone.

"Persimmon? Where are you?" Lira looked around the cave.

"I'm standing right next to you," said Persimmon.

"Where? I can't see you."

"Oh, I must be invisible." Persimmon giggled, having fun with these new powers. She threw the stone into her pocket and plucked another from the bag.

"Can you see me now?" she asked Lira.

"Oh! You frightened me." Lira held her hand up to her face, peeking out from between her fingers.

"Why? It's just me." When Persimmon looked down at her hand, she had long talons and scaled skin. "Oh, I don't like this one at all." She dumped it into her pocket with the others.

"Hurry, they're coming," said Elric, zipping by in a blur. Persimmon turned to see King Sethor dismounting his horse just outside the mouth of the cave. He, Rancor, Filip, and at least a dozen of his guards drew their weapons, looking around as they entered the mouth of the cave. The rest of his army stayed out there.

"Hurry, Persimmon. They are headed this way," cried Lira.

They'd tried so many stones now, but none of them was the right one. Persimmon was starting to worry.

"I only have the one stone left to try. This must be it." She scooped up the last stone, feeling the heat against her palm. Since Elric was still distracting some of the gnomes, and the rest of the cave-dwellers were focused on the food and wine, Sethor and his men were able to sneak into the cave unnoticed.

"Over there!" shouted Rancor, spotting Persimmon and Lira and pointing them out.

"Get them," commanded Sethor.

"You'd better make that last stone work quickly, or we're going to be in a very bad situation," Lira warned her.

"I will. This has to be it." Persimmon rubbed the stone, but no portal appeared. "It didn't work."

"Oh, yes it did, but not in the way we thought. Look," said Lira.

Persimmon turned around to see a large ugly beast that reminded her of a bear with the head of an eagle. It growled and charged toward Sethor. The king and his men fought it while the gnomes scurried around in a frenzy, surprised to see so many inside their cave.

Elric stopped the dog right in front of them. "Persimmon, I can't hold these gnomes off forever. What are you doing? Why haven't you got that portal opened yet?" he asked.

"I've tried all the gemstones, Father, but none of them worked," said Persimmon. "I don't understand it."

"I do," said Elric with a sigh. "The stone that opens and closes the portal must be the one that the thief Rancor still has."

"It figures. What are we going to do?" asked Lira.

"Don't worry. I'll get it." Elric got off the dog and zipped away, heading toward Sethor and the others. It wasn't but a minute before he returned, holding out the last stone to her.

"You are amazing, even for a grouchy little elf," said Persimmon, taking the gem from him. Sure enough, as soon as she touched it, those same swirling colors of blue, pink and orange appeared. They made a circle and grew larger and larger. Then she saw an opening appear, and bright lights coming from within.

"I did it!" cried Persimmon. "I opened the portal. This is so exciting."

She heard a fight going on behind her. Turning to look, she saw Sethor pulling his blade out of the beast that now lay dead. The Blackseed brothers appeared at the mouth of the cave, fighting off the three guards that had entered with Sethor. The rest of his men were outside of the cave, afraid to come in.

"Now!" she heard Stone shout. Stone and Aithrod shot out from behind a rock, managing to surprise Rancor and Filip. "Grab them and head to the portal, quickly, Aithrod. There is no time to lose."

It was a struggle, but since they'd managed to surprise and unarm the Taelgonoth thieves, Stone and Aithrod had no trouble dragging them to the portal. Fang barked and nipped at the heels of the thieves. They were just about to step through the portal when the gnomes started to attack again.

"Dammit, I'll take care of them." Elric jumped atop Fang and started riding around the cave again.

"Quickly, let's go." Stone looked over his shoulder. "Fang, where are you?"

"Elric has him. They're trying to distract the gnomes," Persimmon told him.

"Take good care of Fang, sweetheart. And of yourself as well," said Stone, holding Rancor's arms behind him. "Be sure to close the portal as soon as I get through."

Aithrod entered the portal first with Filip. Stone still held on to Rancor. "I love you, Persimmon and will never forget you."

Tears filled her eyes as Stone took a step through the portal holding Rancor, and disappeared from sight.

"Close the portal. Quickly," shouted Lira. "They're coming!"

She was about to do so when King Sethor pushed past her, diving into the portal, followed by at least six or seven of his men.

"Nay!" she screamed. Sethor had knocked into

her as he passed by her and she'd dropped the gemstone. It rolled along the floor and slipped through the portal as well. "I lost the gemstone. It went through the portal. I need to find it." Persimmon panicked.

"It's too late," Lira told her. "Look. The portal is closing."

Sure enough, to her horror, the portal became smaller and smaller. In another few seconds it would disappear for good. Without that gemstone, she'd have no chance of ever opening the portal again. And that also meant she would never see Stone again either. The man who said he'd loved her would be gone from her life forever.

"I'm going after it," she told Lira, diving toward the portal just as it finished closing. She hit the ground hard, feeling the cold, dusty floor of the cave as the colorful swirling lights disappeared into nothingness over her head.

She was too late!

The portal had closed and taken Stone, the others, and the gemstone with it. Now she had lost the key to making it open again.

"He's gone," she cried, lifting her head from the ground to see nothing but a dark cave in front of her eyes.

Persimmon had failed, and lost Stone Nightstalker forever.

Fifteen

A week had passed and time only made Persimmon angrier at herself for carelessly losing the gemstone that would open up the portal again to hopefully let Stone return. She sat at a table in the courtyard of Evandorm Castle, feeling sad and sorry for herself. She was with Lira. They watched Elric and the Blackseed brothers once again playing cards.

"Your bid, Rhys," said Zann. "And don't even think of using my chickens again."

"I brought my own things to bid this time." Rhys pulled a long black feather out of his bag and reverently laid it on the center of the table.

"What is that?" asked Persimmon, thinking it an odd thing to use as a bid in a game of cards.

"It's the feather of a Stricat," explained Rhys. "It is magical and very rare to have since stricats hardly ever lose their feathers. I was lucky to find it. It's worth a lot."

"Hah! Hardly," said Elric. "I've got at least a

dozen of them at home." Elric swished his hand through the air.

"What is a Stricat?" she asked, not being familiar with this type of animal.

"You probably haven't seen one yet since they keep hidden most of the time," Lira explained. "It is a large wildcat with sharp claws and a shaggy mane and black stripes. It has wings and can also fly."

"That does sound unique," Persimmon answered. "But is it really magical?"

"It can't open a portal if that's what you're asking," said Elric with a grunt. "By the way, the gods are coming down on me hard. I'm going to have to give them back the gemstones, Persimmon. I'm not sure how much longer I can hold them off."

"I'm not giving them to you until I succeed in bringing Stone back to Mura." Her hand went to the pouch that she always carried at her side.

"You've tried each of those stones so many times that I'm surprised you haven't worn them out," said Lira. "Face it, none of them opens a portal."

"I keep thinking there must be a way to open that portal again, even without the gem that was lost." Persimmon yawned, not having had much sleep since she lost Stone. Fang laid at her feet under the table, missing Stone almost as much as she. Persimmon she reached down to pet the dog. They'd been a good comfort to each other, but just seeing the hound made her miss Stone even more.

"We all miss him," said Lira. "But, sister, what happened wasn't your fault."

"At least we got rid of King Sethor and some of

his men," said Zann, placing a basket of Arcine eggs on the table as his bet.

"Not those stinky eggs again," complained Darium. "Don't you have anything else to bid?"

"I don't because my wife keeps me busy watching for a portal to open that's not going to happen. However, she and her sister won't stop trying." Zann yawned too.

"It's a shame you couldn't claim Sethor's kingdom as your own, Darium." Rhys reached out and stroked the feather. "It would be nice if you were a king of Mura too, like me and Zann."

"Yes," agreed Lira. "It would be nice to have all three Blackseed brothers as kings."

"I don't need or want to be a king, so let it go," said Darium. "Besides, you know as well as the rest of us that Sethor's nephew, Sebastian Ravenwolf stepped in to rule Macada Castle once Sethor disappeared through the portal. Sethor's men are loyal to him now and nothing is ever going to change."

"Elric? Your bid?" Zann tapped the table with the edges of his cards to get the elf's attention.

"Hrmph," he snorted and threw down his cards. "I'm out." Even Elric had seemed different lately. He'd been much kinder to Persimmon, and hadn't been his normal cantankerous self continuously. Stone's absence seemed to have affected everyone, even Fang.

The dog laid under the table with his nose between his paws, not even excited to chase a skunet or beg for food. One man's absence seemed to branch out and affect so many.

"I wish I could at least use the gazing orb to scry,"

said Persimmon. "If so, then I'd know if Stone is all right. For all I know he might be dead."

"Don't worry, sister, I'm sure everything will turn out all right in the end." Lira rubbed Persimmon's back with one hand, trying to comfort her.

"I don't see how that will ever happen. I'm not even seeing ghosts anymore. So if Stone's been killed I won't even be able to tell him goodbye that way."

"You worry too much. Just like your mother," said Elric.

"Darium, place your bid," said Zann, holding his cards close to his chest.

"All right." Darium dug into his pouch and slowly slid a ring onto the table. It was the same ring he tried to use in the game the day Persimmon came to Mura.

"Not that old ring again," complained Zann.

"Hey, it's better than Arcine eggs that you happen to be using again as well," said Darium in his defense.

"I still wonder whose ring this was." Rhys picked it up to inspect it.

"Let me see that." Elric snatched it away from Rhys before he could stop him. "Ah ha! I thought it looked familiar."

"What are you saying?" asked Darium. "Don't start telling us again that I stole that from a dead person, because I didn't."

"See this design on the ring?" Elric held it up for the others to see. Persimmon was lost in her thought and paid little attention to the conversation.

"Aye. So what?" asked Zann.

"Now look at that necklace around Persimmon's neck."

Persimmon heard her name and her head snapped up. Her hand went to her necklace and her fingers caressed it. "What are you saying about my necklace?"

"It's the same," said Rhys, peering across the table.

"That proves it. The ring is mine." Elric was at it again, claiming everything as his own.

"Now wait a minute," griped Darium. "You say that about everything."

Fang whimpered from beneath the table.

"It does look like the same design," said Zann. "Persimmon, where did you get that necklace?"

"It was my mother's," she explained. "The nuns brought me her things after she died. I liked it, so I wore it. I also thought it would help me to keep close to my mother."

"I gave Luna that necklace at the same time I gave her this ring when I asked her to marry me," explained Elric.

"What?" Persimmon was shocked to hear this. "But you and Mother never married."

"Nay," said the elf. "She told me she wouldn't marry me because although she loved me, she'd seen in her gazing ball that she was going to die young. She said I should go marry someone else so I wouldn't end up being a widower."

"Mother told you that she loved you?" This surprised Persimmon.

"Yes. And that she would die young, which she kind of did. I guess those gazing balls really don't lie after all," said Elric.

"And you told her that you loved her but she still wouldn't marry you?" continued Persimmon, starting to put things together.

"I could see she was visibly upset. "That is the night I found out she had her lover there."

"King Helix Kapion," mumbled Persimmon.

"Yes, that's right."

"What happened?" asked Lira.

"That thief stole my gemstones as well as the ring that night, and disappeared through a portal. I told Luna what happened but she didn't believe me. She called me a liar and said I was jealous and that she never wanted to see me again."

"Oh, no, I am so sorry," said Persimmon.

"So Rancor must have stolen and ring and dropped it coming through the portal," said Darium. "That's why Murk found it and brought it to me."

"After that, things became bad between me and Luna. Even after you were born, I didn't see you a lot because I honestly wasn't sure you were my child and the last thing I wanted to do was to visit the daughter of that greedy king thief."

"Fine, it's yours. Take the ring," said Darium with a wave of his hand.

Elric looked over at Persimmon for a moment before taking the ring and shoving into his pouch.

"I didn't know you and Mother loved each other. That makes things different," said Persimmon.

"Why?" asked the elf.

"Because, if I am your child then I was conceived out of love, not greed, deceit or hate."

"Like if you were sired by King Kapion," said Zann with a nod.

"Husband, don't say such things," gasped Lira.

"It's all right." Persimmon's hand covered the bag holding her gazing orb. "He's right. I wish now that I had told Stone I loved him before he stepped through the portal."

"I heard him tell you that he loved you," said Lira.

"Yes." Persimmon smiled and rubbed her fingers over the bag. "Even if I never see him again, I will always love him."

Right after she professed her love for Stone aloud while rubbing the gazing orb, she felt heat under her fingers and a slight vibration coming from the bag. "Something is happening." Quickly, she scooped the gazing orb out of the bag and held it up with two hands in front of her.

"Persimmon? What is it?" asked Lira.

"I—I can see something in the orb. Yes, I'm sure of it. I am actually and finally scrying."

"Really?" asked her father. "I wonder what activated your power."

"I know exactly what it was," she told them, smiling even more when Stone's face emerged in the gazing ball. "It was love. My love for Stone and his for me. I guess saying it aloud was the secret."

"Do you really think so?" asked Lira. "How wonderful."

"Yes. I know that's what it was. And that was why Mother was able to scry as well. Father, she loved you and you loved her. I never realized that until now."

"You don't have to call me Father, Persimmon." Elric lowered his head and dragged a lazy finger over the top of the table. "Especially since we don't even know that it is true."

"I want to find out. I am going to find out." She saw another vision in the gazing orb and all hope was restored of seeing Stone again. "I see in the orb that the stone I thought fell through the portal didn't go through after all. It is still there in the cave, lodged under a rock."

She jumped to her feet.

"Where are you going?" asked Lira.

"I have to get back to the cave to find and use that stone. I am going to open the portal and join Stone in his land of Taelgonoth."

S tone had been back in Taelgonoth for a week now, and every day just got worse than the one before. Even after bringing the thieves to his king, justice had not been served. King Helix Kapion was not happy to know that not a single gemstone had been returned. The king was even angrier with Stone when he heard from King Sethor that a witch in Mura had the stones and she had been using them to do magic.

It seemed Sethor had seen Persimmon using the stones trying to open the portal. He told Helix every magical feat she'd accomplished and now Helix wanted the stones more than ever. Stone explained to him that only the Chosen One of the gods could use them. That was a mistake. Because now he wanted Persimmon, too. Especially when he discovered that she was the daughter of the sorceress, Luna.

Stone and Aithrod rode their horses along with the traveling party that consisted of Helix, Sethor, Rancor, Filip and about a dozen of Helix and Sethor's men. They were headed back to the cave where the portal had opened. Every day they took a trip here, waiting for it to open again. Sethor and Helix were good friends now, even though Stone and Aithrod divulged the information of how Sethor wanted to take over Taelgonoth. Of course, Sethor turned the story around, saying he would never do such a thing and Rancor and Filip backed him up. Helix wanted to get back to Mura, and Stone only prayed that if that portal opened again, Sethor's men wouldn't be there waiting on the other side to come through and seize Taelgonoth after all.

They dismounted and walked into the cave. Stone felt saddened knowing he was never going to see Persimmon again. She had said she'd come with him even though he told her not to. He suspected she would do it anyway, but thankfully it had been a week now and she hadn't showed up. That told him that she'd listened to him, after all. And while that made him happy because it secured her safety, it made him sad that they would never end up together. Not to mention, he missed his dog.

"Mayhap Persimmon will come through the portal today," Aithrod whispered.

"She's not coming." Stone's heart ached. "If she were, she'd be here by now."

"You miss her, don't you?"

"I miss her more than you can imagine. I miss Fang, too."

"I miss them as well," said Aithrod, speaking softly so the others couldn't hear them. "We're all alone here now. We really have no one but each other."

"I know that. And I am thinking that we made a

huge mistake in coming back. Aithrod, we should have stayed on Mura where we were happy."

"Stone, what do you think Helix will do with us now? I don't understand why he hasn't put us in the dungeon or killed us already."

"He's probably planning on using us to try to lure Persimmon into opening the portal again somehow. If she does open it and comes through, I pray she doesn't bring the gemstones with her. Ever since I told our addled king only one with magic can use them, he has his mind set on getting them anyway. I just don't understand it."

"I want more than just the gemstones," said Helix, having overheard them. "I want the girl as well."

"Why? If she does come through the portal, I'm warning you not to touch her."

Helix laughed. "If she can truly see the past and future, then she will come here on her own."

"She might come to save me and Aithrod from your clutches, but I assure you she is powerful. She won't put up with the likes of you."

"On the contrary, I believe she will come and it won't be for you two. She'll be coming here to see me."

"Nay, she'd never," spat Stone.

Helix chuckled again. "And when she hears what I have to say, she'll help me instead of hurt me, I promise."

"There is nothing you could possibly say that would make Persimmon want to help you."

"You are wrong," said the king. "She is going to want to stay with me because I am going to tell her the truth. That I am her father."

They had just entered the cave when Stone noticed the shimmering colors swirling around and knew the portal was opening.

"I see it!" shouted Rancor. "Someone is opening the portal from the other side. It's finally happening again."

"Draw your weapons," commanded Sethor, unsheathing his blade.

"Don't hurt my daughter, but kill anyone else who steps through," ordered Helix. "I want the girl unharmed. She is going to be my new secret weapon."

"Persimmon is no one's weapon and she won't be treated that way," shouted Stone.

"You two stand back," commanded Helix. And don't cause me any problems."

"If they do, I'll kill them myself like I should have done the first time they came to see me, snarled Sethor. "I told you not to bring them, Helix. Mayhap we should tie them up. They are not to be trusted."

"Too late," said Helix. "Look, I see someone emerging through the portal now." An evil smile crossed his face, making Stone feel sick since he knew Persimmon was coming through.

To Stone's surprise, instead of Persimmon stepping through, The Blackseed brothers stumbled out of the portal with their weapons drawn.

"Kill them!" shouted Sethor. "They're no friends, I assure you."

A fight started between the brothers and Kings Sethor and Helix. The king had taken away Stone and Aithrod's weapons, so Stone used his bare hands to fight. He'd taken down two of the guards when he saw Persimmon step through the portal next to join them. She was holding out her hands, keeping the portal open.

"Fast, go through the portal," she told Stone and the Blackseeds. "I don't know how much longer I can hold it open."

"Persimmon, stay with me," called out Helix. "You are my daughter and this is where you belong."

"What?" She looked over at Helix and when she did, the portal started to shrink.

"If we're going through, it's now or never," shouted Darium. "The portal is starting to shrink."

"Stone, won't you and Aithrod come to live at Mura?" asked Persimmon, her hands still raised, holding the portal open. "Please. I want you to. We all do."

"You don't have to ask me twice." Aithrod bolted through the portal, disappearing with a snapping sound.

"The rest of you go. I'll hold them off," said Darium, his sword clashing with more of Helix's soldiers who had just entered the cave at hearing the sound of the fight.

"I see the bag of stones. She has them attached to her belt." Filip reached for them, but Sethor struck him down dead.

"The stones are mine," said the greedy Sethor. "And all deals with you are off, thief!"

"Nay, those gems are not yours. They belong to me and my daughter." Helix fought his way over to them. "Persimmon, stay here on Taelgonoth with me. You are the daughter of a king and you deserve everything I can give you. I will treat you like the princess that you truly are."

"Y—you're really my father?" asked Persimmon, getting distracted and seeming extremely shaken. When she lost her focus, the portal started closing more.

"We're going to be trapped here, now get going," Darium told his brothers.

Rhys and Zann jumped through the portal. When Rancor was about to go through, Stone grabbed him, took his sword and threw him to the side.

"Not you," he said. "Mura doesn't want your kind. It'll never be a dark place like Taelgonoth if I can help it."

"We're losing the portal," shouted Darium. "Move quickly."

"Go!" Stone told him. "I'll hold them off and come through with Persimmon."

"Are you sure?" Darium was reluctant to leave. "I left you once before and regretted it later."

"I can handle this. Go on, there is no time to lose," shouted Stone.

"Behind you," yelled Darium. Stone turned in time to see Rancor charging him with a knife in his hand. Stone took him down with his sword, killing the man instantly.

"All right. I'm going. Now follow me through. We'll wait on the other side with our weapons in case anyone else comes through with you." Darium backed up to the portal with his blade still drawn, and stepped back and through the portal leading to Mura.

"Give me the stones, or I'll kill you." Sethor grabbed Persimmon and put a blade to her throat.

Her hands lowered and the portal became less vibrant.

"No, not again," mumbled Stone, seeing Sethor threaten Persimmon's life for the second time now. He was about to save her when something else happened.

"Those stones are mine!" Helix bolted forward, sinking his blade into Sethor's back. King Sethor fell to the ground with blood spurting out from his mouth and his eyes bulging. If Stone wasn't already certain that Helix's soul was too dark to be saved, he certainly was now. What kind of a man would stab another in the back without giving him a chance to defend himself? This man was greedier and even more evil than Mura's King Sethor. He knew that now.

"Persimmon, quickly. We need to go." With his blade still pointed outward, he grabbed her hand, meaning to go through, but she pulled away.

"Wait," she told him.

"Persimmon? What are you doing?"

"Stone, I came here not only to get you but to find my true father." Her gaze traveled back to the king.

"And now you have found me, daughter," said Helix, holding out his hand. "Come with me. Let us go back to my castle where you belong."

"Nay!" shouted Stone, fighting off another guard. "Don't do it. Persimmon, he is evil. He just wants you for your stones and powers."

"I'm confused," she said, looking at him with tears streaming down her face. "Stone, this might be my true father. If so, I'd like to get to know him."

"Nay, you don't want to know him. I assure you, he is evil. Walk away now while you still can."

"Come, Persimmon. I've been trying to get to you since that night your mother and I conceived you. There is so much I want to tell you."

"That's a lie, Persimmon," Stone warned her. "He didn't even know you were born until I foolishly mentioned it when I returned."

"Oh, Stone. I have lived my life without a true father. It has been a hole in my heart. Mayhap you should go without me."

"I won't do that," he said. "You are coming with me and not staying here. You're confused. I won't let you do it."

"You can't give her the life she deserves, but I can," said the king, walking forward, still holding out his hand. "Come, daughter. We have many years to make up for."

"F—Father?" asked Persimmon, tears streaming down her cheeks.

"That's right," the king answered with a smile.

"Did you love my mother, Luna?" she asked, surprising Stone that now is the time she chose to ask that.

The king stopped and blink. "Why would you ask that? What does it matter?"

"I need to know. Did you love her when you coupled with her?"

"Don't be silly," spat the king, laughing. "No man truly loves his wife. It's unheard of. Besides, I wasn't married to Luna. We were just having a little fun."

"Persimmon, please. I can't hold them off much

longer and the portal is closing," cried Stone, still fighting off man after man.

"She's coming with me." The king grabbed her hand and pulled her to him.

"Naaaay!" cried Stone. "I love her. And even if I can't give her all that you can, I will still treat her like a princess with my love."

"That is nonsense and means nothing," yelled the king.

"Well, it means the world to me." Persimmon used her powers to throw the king across the room. And when a slew of his guards rushed forward with their blades drawn, she used her mind power to stop them, pushing them away as well.

"I love you, Stone, and I believe we can be very happy together." She took his hand in hers. "Let's go home."

They stepped through the portal together just as it closed. Since they'd barely made it, they were thrown to the ground with force as the portal snapped closed and disappeared behind them.

"We made it. We're back." Stone looked up smiling, but then he groaned. "Oh, no. I forgot about the damned gnomes."

Whooping and hollering, dozens of gnomes sped forward and rappelled down from the cave roof. Each of them had their weapon of choice, and they were all aimed directly at Stone.

"Get up, sweetheart. Hurry." He pulled Persimmon to her feet. "We've got to get out of this cave. We're being attacked by gnomes."

"Don't worry about that," she said with a smile. "Father. Fang? Can you help us out?"

"What?" asked Stone, turning to see the crazy elf sitting atop Stone's dog.

"I could use my powers to rid us of the gnomes, but I'm afraid I might hurt them," Persimmon told him. "I think this way is much better."

Elric bolted around the room atop the dog and the gnomes ran in fright. Elric shouted nonsense and Fang barked.

"Good to see you, Fang," said Stone, laughing.

"We've got everything handled," she said with a wink, reaching up to kiss him.

"Yes, I can see that. Everything is exactly how it should be." He kissed her back and took her hand, heading out of the cave. Damn, it felt good to be back on Mura.

Seventeen

Stone and Persimmon were married a week later in Glint, the home of the elves. The Blackseed brothers and their families were there as well as Alaina the Queen of the Fae, and Lira's Aunt Sasha who was the Elven Queen since Lira now ruled with her husband at Evandorm Castle.

"I knew you two would marry all along," said Lira as they sat down at a long table in the courtyard for a feast. Lira had served as Persimmon's maid of honor and Aithrod was Stone's best man. Fang had walked down the aisle carrying a small box that had the ring in it that Elric had once given to Luna. Elric said he wanted Persimmon to have it as a remembrance of her mother, even if he and Luna had never been married. It still was a symbol of their love for each other.

"So, are the two of you ever going to want to go back to Taelgonoth?" asked Darium, smiling because he already knew the answer.

"Never," Stone answered. "Aithrod and I decided that Mura is our home now." Stone helped Persimmon to get seated and then reached down and petted Fang on the head. "Fang likes it better here, too.

"I was talking about you and Persimmon," said Darium.

"Yes, Persimmon, you never told us how you felt when King Kapion told you he was your father," said Talia, holding on to Darium's arm. "Don't you want to go back to get to know him?"

Persimmon looked over to Elric who sadly sat by himself, not even looking up. Ever since she had come through the portal and told everyone that King Kapion was really her father, Elric had become distant and sad. She didn't like seeing him this way. She had always wished for the presence of a father in her life, and now that she finally got what she wanted she realized it wasn't important anymore.

"King Helix Kapion is an evil man, just like my husband has said." Persimmon reached over and kissed Stone. "So, nay, I don't ever want to go back to Taelgonoth. Here is where I belong."

"It's a shame, sister, that you finally discovered you are a princess and now can't do anything about it." Lira sat down and her daughter Valindra climbed up on her lap.

"The only princess I want to be is the one I'll be in Stone's eyes." Persimmon smiled and they kissed again. She looked up to see Elric slipping away. He seemed so sad that her heart was breaking.

"Elric, please come join us," she called out. "I have something for you."

"What?" The elf looked up in confusion.

Persimmon reached down and unclasped the bag of gemstones at her side and held it out. "I'd like to give the gemstones to you."

"Why?" asked the elf. "Only the Chosen One, which is you, can use them. I'm sure you don't want to give up all those powers." He shuffled over. It was so odd to see the elf moving so slowly since he always zipped around at a high speed. The man seemed to be giving up all hope. He no longer had a spark of life within him.

"I don't need them," said Persimmon. "I want you to take them and give them back to the gods of Mura instead."

"You do?" He approached the table, looking at her in question. "Why would you do such a thing?"

"So they can forgive you and so they will never take away your powers. Plus, we need you as sage of Mura. You are the wisest man we know." She reached out and took his hands, tucking the bag between them.

"All right," he said, and sighed. "Thank you."

"Did Elric just say thank you?" she heard Rhys ask.

"He never says that. He must be sick," Zann answered.

"Sister, where will you and Stone be staying now that you are married?" asked Lira.

"Well, I had hoped we'd be welcome here in Glint."

"In the home of the elves?" asked Elric, looking up in surprise. "Why in the world would you want to stay here since you found out you are not even part elf?"

"I want to stay here to be close to my father," she said with a big smile.

"What?" Elric wrinkled his nose as if he'd smelled something fowl. "Your father is in Taelgonoth, not Mura."

"Nay, that's not true," she told him.

"Persimmon? What are you saying?" asked Stone, obviously wondering where she was going with this.

"Since Stone and I professed our love for each other I've been able to scry using the gazing crystal. I am getting good at it and have seen a lot of things."

"So what?" asked Elric.

"So I am going to try something, just to make sure."

"What does that mean?" Elric didn't seem at all interested.

She pulled out the gazing orb and held it up in her hands. "I am now going to ask a question, and the gazing orb will show me the true answer."

"That's nice." Elric sighed again and tied the bag of stones onto his belt.

"Gazing orb, I want to see a vision of my father. My true father."

Elric sighed again and looked at the ground.

"Is it working?" asked Medea excitedly since no one but Persimmon could see the visions within it.

"It is," she said with a nod. "And I see...you, Elric! King Helix Kapion is not my true father after all. But you are!"

"I am?" Elric's head snapped up. "Are you sure about that?" He looked at her in a suspicious manner.

"Mother always told me that the gazing ball

doesn't lie," she said, not directly answering his question.

"So, I'm your father then?" A smile spread across his face. "You're half-elf, even though you don't have pointy ears?"

"That's right. I think I must have inherited more of my mother's looks instead."

"Thank the gods," said Darium under his breath.

"You did?" Elric's face got brighter and happiness spread up into his eyes now.

"I suppose it is possible," said Stone with a nod.

"Daughter. You're my daughter! I have two daughters now, as well as two sons. Yippee! I'm going to the pyramids of the gods right now to give them back the stones. I want the gods to smile on me from now on. I also want to be on my best behavior and be the best father ever."

"You'll have to be the best grandfather as well. And I'm not talking about Lira's children." Persimmon put her hand on her belly and looked over to see Stone's very surprised look on his face.

"What are you saying?" asked Elric. "There is no way you are already pregnant. You haven't even known Stone long enough."

"What are you saying, sweetheart?" asked Stone, putting his arm around Persimmon's shoulders and pulling her closer.

"I am not pregnant yet, but the gazing orb has shown me that I will be with child very soon," Persimmon answered, and giggled. "I actually can't wait."

"And neither can I," added Stone with a big smile.

"Oh, I've got so much to do. We need to prepare

for the baby," said Elric. "I hope the little tyke at least gets my ears and not the big oaf's ugly nose. That would be nasty." He was speaking about Stone and everyone there knew it.

"Now wait a minute, I'm not a big oaf," said Stone in his defense.

"It looks like Elric's accepted you now, Stone. You've joined the rest of us big oafs, so welcome to the family," shouted Zann, making everyone laugh and cheer since Elric always called the Blackseed boys the same thing.

"I'll see you later." Elric sped off in a blur, still whooping and hollering in joy.

"Can you look into your gazing orb and see if we're going to have a boy or a girl?" asked Stone, nuzzling her neck and kissing her behind the ear.

"Nay, it doesn't work that way, Stone." She put the orb back into her pouch. "I can't ask the orb questions. It only shows me what it wants me to see."

"What?" He pulled back and looked at her in question. "But you just told Elric that you asked to see your true father and you saw him. And you said we'd have a child soon."

"I did say those things, didn't I." She smiled deviously.

"Persimmon?" He looked at her in a scolding manner. "Are you lying about being able to scry again? The same way you were when you first got to Mura? Because, remember how much trouble that got you into."

"The answer to your question is yes and no," she told him. "I really can scry now, and I am thankful that our love awakened the crystal's magic." She reached up and kissed him.

"But you only told Elric what he wanted to hear, right?" he said, tapping his finger against her lips. "That is being a naughty girl. Plus, you told me what I wanted to hear as well."

"Elric was so forlorn. Didn't you see the way he perked up once he thought he had sired me?"

"Still, that was being dishonest. I'm not sure you should have done that."

"Well, we only have King Kapion's word to go on that he is really my father. So, I'm not sure that Elric didn't really sire me after all. No one knows the truth. My mother didn't even seem to know."

"Well, you don't look like you have an ounce of elven blood in you."

"Weren't you the one who just agreed that it was possible that I inherited more of my mother's looks instead?"

"Mmm hmm," he said, still giving her the scolding eye. "Because I wanted to support you."

"And you knew it was want Elric wanted to hear," she said with a knowing nod.

"Well, it could be true. I mean, yes, it could have happened."

"Stone, you need to remember something. I never even knew about King Kapion before I came here to Mura. However, I grew up thinking Elric was my father for the last twenty-five years. Granted, Elric wasn't all that kind to me, and didn't visit me but a few times in my life. Still, those few visits meant something to me. It gave me hope. Hope that someday I would have a relationship with him the same way that others do with their fathers."

"You mean like Elric has with Lira?"

"Yes."

"But you don't."

"Not yet, but these things take time. And remember, Lira didn't get along with Elric either until recently."

"I'm not surprised. I don't know how anyone can really tolerate that man."

"Stone, that's my father you're speaking of. Please, be nice."

"Yes, I suppose I can see your point. I think mayhap you might be Elric's daughter, after all. Or, at least, I'd like to think so. Even if the man is irritating, he's a much better choice of a father than King Kapion who never had and never will have love in his heart."

"I agree. So, I have to go with the one man that I feel in my heart is the one who sired me. After all, I am sure I was born on love and not hate and lust."

"Me, too."

"Persimmon, are you sure you will never want to go back to Taelgonoth to talk to King Kapion again?"

"Never. And just to make sure I won't be tempted, is one of the reasons I gave the stones back to Elric. I don't ever want that portal to Taelgonoth opened again."

"Good idea."

"Will you miss your home, Stone?"

"Nay. I have no one there anymore. Everyone I care about is here in Mura. Besides, this is my home now, Persimmon. With you. In Mura."

"Yes. And Elric is my father now and will always be. That is all that matters. I have no need to look any further. I have found everything I have ever longed for right here. Especially you, Stone. I wouldn't give that up for anything."

"I am only thankful that the portal brought us together in the first place." He hugged her. Fang's head came up between them, looking for food.

They both laughed.

"I never expected that the sky would open up one day and the man I would marry would fall atop me and knock me to the ground, but it happened, didn't it?"

"Yes, it certainly did, sweetheart. If that's not a sure sign that we belong together, then I don't know what is."

"I propose a toast," Lira called out, holding up her goblet of wine. "To my new sister, Persimmon and her husband, Stone. May they always be as happy and as in love as there are right now."

"I'll drink to that." Stone raised his glass and so did Persimmon.

"Stone, tell us how you feel being married to Persimmon?" asked Aithrod.

"Well, I feel lucky and loved and as if I've met someone special who I almost didn't meet. I feel as if everything bad that happened really happened for a reason and if it didn't, Persimmon and I never would have met, being from two different lands only connected by a portal. I also feel as if my new life will be so much better than my old one. I have so much to be thankful for. Not only being a husband to the woman I love, but also looking forward to one day becoming a father and raising a child even though I don't know the first thing about raising children but I am willing to learn."

"Egads, the man is a windbag." Elric was back from the pyramids of the gods already and standing in front of the table holding up a goblet of wine as well.

"Father, did the gods forgive you?" asked Persimmon.

"Of course, they did," said Elric. "Stone, if you're going to be married to my daughter, I'm going to insist you don't talk everyone to death like you're doing now."

"Father, that's not nice," said Persimmon, smiling all the while she spoke.

"He's right, you know. We're hungry so let's get this over with, can we?" called out Zann, always anxious to eat.

"Just sum it all up. Give us one word to describe how you're feeling, Stone, and then let's eat." Darium held up his goblet and waited. They all did.

Stone looked back at Persimmon and smiled widely. "All right. One word, let me think.

"Just say anything, Stone," whispered Persimmon. "Everyone is waiting."

"Nay, I want to make sure it explains exactly how I feel, sweetheart."

"All right. Take your time."

"I don't have to. I know the answer now." He raised his goblet higher. "The one word to describe being married to Persimmon would have to be no other than **Charmed**!

I hope you enjoyed the tale of Persimmon and Stone and will take a moment to leave a review for me.

My love of fantasy and the paranormal is what inspired me to create the land of Mura which is featured in my Portals of Destiny Series. If you'd like to see a full, color map of the land with all the places mentioned in the books, you can do so by visiting my website at https://elizabethrosenovels.com. Be sure to sign up for my newsletter while you are there.

You can follow me on **Amazon**, **Bookbub**, **Goodreads**, **Facebook** and **Twitter**. I also have a **Private Readers' Group** on Facebook that I invite you to join.

In case you have missed the stories of Darium, Rhys and Zann Blackseed, here are the books that come before Charmed.

Portals of Destiny

Bedeviled
Bewitched

Beguiled

Or just see the entire series.

For a special treat, pick up the books in audio as well.

And if you'd like to read about more of the fae folk, be sure to read my **Elemental Magick Series** where some of the elemental fae who made guest appearances in the books have their stories to tell as well.

Thank you, and I wish you all a magical, mystical life!

Elizabeth Rose

About Elizabeth

Elizabeth Rose is an award-winning, bestselling author of over 100 books and counting. She writes medieval, historical, contemporary, paranormal, and western romance. Her books are available as EBooks, paperbacks, and some audiobooks as well.

Her favorite characters in her works include dark, dangerous and tortured heroes, and feisty, independent heroines who know how to wield a sword. She loves writing 14th century medieval novels, and is well-known for her many series.

Elizabeth loves the outdoors. In the summertime, you can find her in her secret garden with her laptop, swinging in her hammock working on her next book. Elizabeth is a born storyteller and passionate about sharing her works with her readers.

Please be sure to visit her website at **Elizabethrosenovels.com** to read excerpts from any of her novels and get sneak peeks at covers of upcoming books. You can follow her on **Twitter**, **Facebook**, **Goodreads** or **BookBub**. Join Elizabeth's **newsletter** so you don't miss out on new releases or upcoming events.